OTHER BOOKS BY ROALD DAHL

The Wonderful Story of Henry Sugar

AND SIX MORE

The Wonderful Story of Henry Sugar

AND SIX MORE

by ROALD DAHL

Alfred A. Knopf / New York

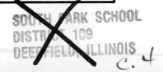

THIS IS A BORZOI BOOK PUBLISHED BY ALFRED A. KNOPF, INC.

Copyright 1945, 1947, 1952 © 1977 by Roald Dahl.
All rights reserved under International and Pan-American Copyright
Conventions. Published in the United States by Alfred A. Knopf, Inc.,
New York, and simultaneously in Canada by Random House of Canada
Limited, Toronto. Distributed by Random House, Inc., New York.
Manufactured in the United States of America.

"A Piece of Cake" was first published in *The Saturday Evening Post* as
"Shot Down in Libya"; "The Mildenhall Treasure" was first published in
The Saturday Evening Post as "He Ploughed Up $1,000,000"; and part of
"The Wonderful Story of Henry Sugar" was originally published in
Argosy as "The Amazing Eyes of Kuda Bux". "The Hitchhiker"
was first published in *Atlantic Monthly*.

The photographs following page 71 are reproduced
by kind permission of the British Library Board.

Library of Congress Cataloging in Publication Data

Dahl, Roald. The wonderful story of Henry Sugar and six more.
CONTENTS: The boy who talked with animals—The hitchhiker—The
Mildenhall treasure—The swan—The wonderful story of Henry Sugar—
Lucky break—A piece of cake.
[1. Short stories] I. Title. PZ7.D15151St3 [Fic] 77-5354
ISBN 0-394-83604-9 ISBN 0-394-93604-3 lib. bdg. 0 9 8 7 6 5

This book is dedicated with affection and sympathy
to all young people
(including my own son and three daughters)
who are going through that long and difficult
metamorphosis when they are no longer children
and have not yet become adults.

Contents

The Boy Who Talked
with Animals

Not so long ago, I decided to spend a few days in the West Indies. I was to go there for a short holiday. Friends had told me it was marvelous. I would laze around all day long, they said, sunning myself on the silver beaches and swimming in the warm green sea.

I chose Jamaica, and flew direct from London to Kingston. The drive from Kingston airport to my hotel on the north shore took two hours. My room in the hotel had a little balcony, and from there I could step straight down onto the beach. There were tall coconut palms growing all around, and every so often an enormous green nut the size of a football would fall out of the sky and drop with a thud on the sand. It was considered foolish to linger underneath a coconut palm because if one of those things landed on your head, it would smash your skull.

The Jamaican girl who came in to tidy my room told me that a wealthy American called Mr. Wasserman had met his end in precisely that manner only two months before.

"You're joking," I said to her.

"Not joking!" she cried. "No, *suh!* I sees it happening with my very own eyes!"

"But wasn't there a terrific fuss about it?" I asked.

"They hush it up," she answered darkly. "The hotel folks hush it up and so do the newspaper folks because things like that are very bad for the tourist business."

"And you say you actually saw it happen?"

"I actually saw it happen," she said. "Mr. Wasserman, he's standing right under that very tree over there on the beach. He's got his camera out and he's pointing it at the sunset. It's a red sunset that evening, and very pretty. Then all at once, down comes a big green nut right smack onto the top of his bald head, *wham!* And that," she added with a touch of relish, "is the very last sunset, Mr. Wasserman ever did see."

"You mean it killed him instantly?"

"I don't know about *instantly*," she said. "I remember the next thing that happens the camera falls out of his hands onto the sand. Then his arms drop down to his sides and hang there. Then he starts swaying. He sways backward and forward several times ever so gentle, and I'm standing there watching him, and I says to myself the poor man's gone all dizzy and maybe he's going to faint any moment. Then very very slowly, he keels right over and down he goes."

"Was he dead?"

"Dead as a doornail," she said.

"Good heavens."

"That's right," she said. "It never pays to be standing under a coconut palm when there's a breeze blowing."

"Thank you," I said. "I'll remember that."

On the evening of my second day, I was sitting on my little balcony with a book on my lap and a tall glass of rum punch in my hand. I wasn't reading the book. I was watching a small green lizard stalking another small green lizard on the balcony floor about six feet away. The stalking lizard was coming up on the other one from behind, moving forward very slowly and very cautiously, and when he came within reach, he flicked out a long tongue and touched the other one's tail. The other one jumped round, and the two of them faced each other, motionless, glued to the floor, crouching, staring, and very tense. Then suddenly, they started doing a funny little hopping dance together. They hopped up in the

air. They hopped backward. They hopped forward. They
hopped sideways. They circled one another like two boxers,
hopping and prancing and dancing all the time. It was a
queer thing to watch, and I guessed it was some sort of a
courtship ritual they were going through. I kept very still,
waiting to see what was going to happen next.

But I never saw what happened next because at that
moment I became aware of a great commotion on the beach
below. I glanced over and saw a crowd of people clustering
around something at the water's edge. There was a narrow
canoe-type fisherman's boat pulled up on the sand nearby,
and all I could think of was that the fisherman had come
in with a lot of fish and that the crowd was looking at it.

A haul of fish is something that has always fascinated
me. I put my book aside and stood up. More people were
trooping down from the hotel veranda and hurrying over
the beach to join the crowd on the edge of the water. The
men were wearing those frightful Bermuda shorts that come
down to the knees, and their shirts were bilious with pinks
and oranges and every other clashing color you could think
of. The women had better taste, and were dressed for the
most part in pretty cotton dresses. Nearly everyone carried
a drink in one hand.

I picked up my own drink and stepped down from the
balcony onto the beach. I made a little detour around the
coconut palm under which Mr. Wasserman had supposedly
met his end and strode across the beautiful silvery sand to
join the crowd.

But it wasn't a haul of fish they were staring at. It was
a turtle, an upside-down turtle lying on its back in the sand.
But what a turtle it was! It was a giant, a mammoth. I had
not thought it possible for a turtle to be as enormous as this.
How can I describe its size? Had it been the right way up,
I think a tall man could have sat on its back without his

feet touching the ground. It was perhaps five feet long and four feet across, with a high domed shell of great beauty.

The fisherman who had caught it had tipped it onto its back to stop it from getting away. There was also a thick rope tied around the middle of its shell, and one proud fisherman, slim and black and naked except for a small loin-cloth, stood a short way off holding the end of the rope with both hands.

Upside down it lay, this magnificent creature, with its four thick flippers waving frantically in the air, and its long wrinkled neck stretching far out of its shell. The flippers had large sharp claws on them.

"Stand back, ladies and gentlemen, please!" cried the fisherman. "Stand well back! Them claws is *dangerous*, man! They'll rip your arm clear away from your body!"

The crowd of hotel guests was thrilled and delighted by this spectacle. A dozen cameras were out and clicking away. Many of the women were squealing with pleasure and clutching onto the arms of their men, and the men were demonstrating their lack of fear and their masculinity by making foolish remarks in loud voices.

"Make yourself a nice pair of horn-rimmed spectacles out of that shell, hey Al?"

"Darn thing must weigh over a ton!"

"You mean to say it can actually float?"

"Sure it floats. Powerful swimmer, too. Pull a boat easy."

"He's a snapper, is he?"

"That's no snapper. Snapper turtles don't grow as big as that. But I'll tell you what. He'll snap your hand off quick enough if you get too close to him."

"Is that true?" one of the women asked the fisherman. "Would he snap off a person's hand?"

"He would right now," the fisherman said, smiling with brilliant white teeth. "He won't ever hurt you when he's in the ocean, but you catch him and pull him ashore and tip him up like this, then man alive, you'd better watch out! He'll snap at anything that comes in reach!"

"I guess I'd get a bit snappish myself," the woman said, "if I was in his situation."

One idiotic man had found a plank of driftwood on the sand, and he was carrying it toward the turtle. It was a fair-sized plank, about five feet long and maybe an inch thick. He started poking one end of it at the turtle's head.

"I wouldn't do that," the fisherman said. "You'll only make him madder than ever."

When the end of the plank touched the turtle's neck, the great beast whipped around and the mouth opened wide and *snap*, it took the plank in its mouth and bit through it as if it were made of cheese.

"Wow!" they shouted. "Did you see that! I'm glad it wasn't my arm!"

"Leave him alone," the fisherman said. "It don't help to get him all stirred up."

A paunchy man with wide hips and very short hairy legs came up to the fisherman and said, "Listen, feller. I want that shell. I'll buy it from you." And to his plump wife, he said, "You know what I'm going to do, Mildred? I'm going to take that shell home and have it polished up by an expert. Then I'm going to place it smack in the center of our living room! Won't that be something?"

"Fantastic," the plump wife said. "Go ahead and buy it, baby."

"Don't worry," he said. "It's mine already." And to the fisherman, he said, "How much for the shell?"

"I already sold him," the fisherman said. "I sold him shell and all."

"Not so fast, feller," the paunchy man said. "I'll bid you higher. Come on. What'd he offer you?"

"No can do," the fisherman said. "I already sold him."

"Who to?" the paunchy man said.

"To the manager."

"What manager?"

"The manager of the hotel."

"Did you hear that?" shouted another man. "He's sold it to the manager of our hotel! And you know what that means? It means turtle soup, that's what it means!"

"Right you are! And turtle steak! You ever have turtle steak, Bill?"

"I never have, Jack. But I can't wait."

"A turtle steak's better than a beefsteak if you cook it right. It's more tender and it's got one heck of a flavor."

"Listen," the paunchy man said to the fisherman. "I'm not trying to buy the meat. The manager can have the meat. He can have everything that's inside including the teeth and toenails. All I want is the shell."

"And if I know you, baby," his wife said, beaming at him, "you're going to get the shell."

I stood there listening to the conversation of these human beings. They were discussing the destruction, the consumption and the flavor of a creature who seemed, even when upside down, to be extraordinarily dignified. One thing was certain. He was senior to any of them in age. For probably one hundred and fifty years he had been cruising in the green waters of the West Indies. He was there when George Washington was President of the United States and Napoleon was being clobbered at Waterloo. He would have been a small turtle then, but he was most certainly there.

And now he was here, upside down on the beach, waiting to be translated into soup and steak. He was clearly alarmed by all the noise and the shouting around him. His old wrinkled neck was straining out of its shell, and the great head was twisting this way and that as though searching for someone who would explain the reason for all this ill-treatment.

"How are you going to get him up to the hotel?" the paunchy man asked.

"Drag him up the beach with the rope," the fisherman answered. "The staff'll be coming along soon to take him. It's going to need ten men, all pulling at once."

"Hey, listen!" cried a muscular young man. "Why don't *we* drag him up?" The muscular young man was wearing magenta and pea-green Bermuda shorts and no shirt. He had an exceptionally hairy chest, and the absence of a shirt was obviously a calculated touch. "What say we do a little work for our supper?" he cried, rippling his muscles. "Come on, fellers! Who's for some exercise?"

"Great idea!" they shouted. "Splendid scheme!"

The men handed their drinks to the women and rushed to catch hold of the rope. They ranged themselves along it as though for a tug-of-war, and the hairy-chested man appointed himself anchorman and captain of the team.

"Come on, now, fellers!" he shouted. "When I say *heave*, then all heave at once, you understand?"

The fisherman didn't like this much. "It's better you leave this job for the hotel," he said.

"Nonsense!" shouted hairy-chest. "*Heave,* boys, *heave!*"

They all heaved. The giant turtle wobbled on its back and nearly toppled over.

"Don't tip him!" yelled the fisherman. "You're going to tip him over if you do that! And if he gets back onto his legs again, he'll escape for sure!"

"Cool it, laddie," said hairy-chest in a patronizing voice. "How can he escape? We've got a rope round him, haven't we?"

"That old turtle will drag the whole lot of you away with him if you give him a chance!" cried the fisherman. "He'll drag you into the ocean, every one of you!"

"*Heave!*" shouted hairy-chest, ignoring the fisherman. "*Heave,* boys, *heave!*"

And now the gigantic turtle began very slowly to slide up the beach toward the hotel, toward the kitchens, toward the place where the big knives were kept. The womenfolk and the older, fatter, less athletic men followed alongside, shouting encouragement.

"*Heave!*" shouted the hairy-chested anchorman. "Put your back into it, fellers! You can pull harder than that!"

Suddenly I heard screams. Everyone heard them. They were screams so high-pitched, so shrill and so urgent they cut right through everything. "No-o-o-o-o!" screamed the scream. "No! No! No! No! No!"

The crowd froze. The tug-of-war men stopped tugging and the onlookers stopped shouting and every single person present turned toward the place where the screams were coming from.

Half walking, half running down the beach from the hotel were three people, a man, a woman and a small boy. They were half running because the boy was pulling the man along. The man had the boy by the wrist, trying to slow him down, but the boy kept pulling. At the same time, he was jumping and twisting and wriggling and trying to free himself from the father's grip. It was the boy who was screaming.

"Don't!" he screamed. "Don't do it! Let him go! Please let him go!"

The woman, his mother, was trying to catch hold of the boy's other arm to help restrain him, but the boy was jumping about so much, she didn't succeed.

"Let him go!" screamed the boy. "It's horrible what you're doing! Please let him go!"

"Stop that, David!" the mother said, still trying to catch

his other arm. "Don't be so childish! You're making a perfect fool of yourself."

"Daddy!" the boy screamed. "Daddy! Tell them to let him go!"

"I can't do that, David," the father said. "It isn't any of our business."

The tug-of-war pullers remained motionless, still holding the rope with the gigantic turtle on the end of it. Everyone stood silent and surprised, staring at the boy. They were all a bit off balance now. They had the slightly hangdog air of people who have been caught doing something that was not entirely honorable.

"Come on now, David," the father said, pulling against the boy. "Let's go back to the hotel and leave these people alone."

"I'm not going back!" the boy shouted. "I don't want to go back! I want them to let it go!"

"Now, David," the mother said.

"Beat it, kid," the hairy-chested man told the boy.

"You're horrible and cruel!" the boy shouted. "All of you are horrible and cruel!" He threw the words high and shrill at the forty or fifty adults standing there on the beach, and nobody, not even the hairy-chested man, answered him this time. "Why don't you put him back in the sea?" the boy shouted. "He hasn't done anything to you! Let him go!"

The father was embarrassed by his son, but he was not ashamed of him. "He's crazy about animals," he said, addressing the crowd. "Back home he's got every kind of animal under the sun. He talks with them."

"He loves them," the mother said.

Several people began shuffling their feet around in the sand. Here and there in the crowd it was possible to sense a slight change of mood, a feeling of uneasiness, a touch even of shame. The boy, who could have been no more than eight or nine years old, had stopped struggling with his father now. The father still held him by the wrist, but he was no longer restraining him.

"Go on!" the boy called out. "Let him go! Undo the rope and let him go!" He stood very small and erect, facing the crowd, his eyes shining like two stars and the wind blowing in his hair. He was magnificent.

"There's nothing we can do, David," the father said gently. "Let's go on back."

"No!" the boy cried out, and at that moment he suddenly gave a twist and wrenched his wrist free from the father's grip. He was away like a streak, running across the sand toward the giant upturned turtle.

"David!" the father yelled, starting after him. "Stop! Come back!"

The boy dodged and swerved through the crowd like a player running with the ball, and the only person who sprang forward to intercept him was the fisherman. "Don't you go near that turtle, boy!" he shouted as he made a lunge for the swiftly running figure. But the boy dodged round him and kept going. "He'll bite you to pieces!" yelled the fisherman. "Stop, boy! Stop!"

But it was too late to stop him now, and as he came running straight at the turtle's head, the turtle saw him, and the huge upside-down head turned quickly to face him.

The voice of the boy's mother, the stricken, agonized wail of the mother's voice rose up into the evening sky. *"David!"* it cried. *"Oh, David!"* And a moment later, the boy was throwing himself onto his knees in the sand and flinging his arms around the wrinkled old neck and hugging the creature to his chest. The boy's cheek was pressing against the turtle's head, and his lips were moving, whispering soft words that nobody else could hear. The turtle became absolutely still. Even his giant flippers stopped waving in the air.

A great sigh, a long soft sigh of relief went up from the crowd. Many people took a pace or two backward, as though trying perhaps to get a little farther away from something that was beyond their understanding. But the father and mother came forward together and stood about ten feet away from their son.

"Daddy!" the boy cried out, still caressing the old brown head. "Please do something, Daddy! Please make them let him go!"

"Can I be of any help here?" said a man in a white suit who had just come down from the hotel. This, as everyone knew, was Mr. Edwards, the manager. He was a tall, beak-nosed Englishman with a long, pink face. "*What* an extraordinary thing!" he said, looking at the boy and the turtle. "He's lucky he hasn't had his head bitten off." And to the boy, he said, "You'd better come away from there now, sonny. That thing's dangerous."

"I want them to let him go!" cried the boy, still cradling the head in his arms. "Tell them to let him go!"

"You realize he could be killed any moment," the manager said to the boy's father.

"Leave him alone," the father said.

"Rubbish," the manager said. "Go in and grab him. But be quick. And be careful."

"No," the father said.

"What do you mean, no?" said the manager. "These things are lethal! Don't you understand that?"

"Yes," the father said.

"Then for heaven's sake, man, get him away!" cried the manager. "There's going to be a very nasty accident if you don't."

"Who owns it?" the father said. "Who owns the turtle?"

"We do," the manager said. "The hotel has bought it."

"Then do me a favor," the father said. "Let me buy it from you."

The manager looked at the father but said nothing.

"You don't know my son," the father said, speaking quietly. "He'll go crazy if it's taken up to the hotel and slaughtered. He'll become hysterical."

"Just pull him away," the manager said. "And be quick about it."

"He loves animals," the father said. "He really loves them. He communicates with them."

The crowd was silent, trying to hear what was being said. Nobody moved away. They stood as though hypnotized.

"If we let it go," the manager said, "they'll only catch it again."

"Perhaps they will," the father said. "But those things can swim."

"I know they can swim," the manager said. "They'll catch him all the same. This is a valuable item, you must realize that. The shell alone is worth a lot of money."

"I don't care about the cost," the father said. "Don't worry about that. I want to buy it."

The boy was still kneeling in the sand beside the turtle, caressing its head.

The manager took a handkerchief from his breast pocket and started wiping his fingers. He was not keen to let the turtle go. He probably had the dinner menu already planned. On the other hand, he didn't want another gruesome accident on his private beach this season. Mr. Wasserman and the coconut, he told himself, had been quite enough for one year, thank you very much.

The father said, "I would deem it a great personal favor, Mr. Edwards, if you would let me buy it. And I promise you won't regret it. I'll make quite sure of that."

The manager's eyebrows went up just a fraction of an inch. He had got the point. He was being offered a bribe. That was a different matter. For a few seconds he went on wiping his hands with the handkerchief. Then he shrugged his shoulders and said, "Well, I suppose if it will make your boy feel any better . . ."

"Thank you," the father said.

"Oh, thank you!" the mother cried. "Thank you so very much!"

"Willy," the manager said, beckoning to the fisherman.

The fisherman came forward. He looked thoroughly confused. "I never seen anything like this before in my whole life," he said. "This old turtle was the fiercest I ever caught! He fought like a devil when we brought him in! It took all six of us to land him! That boy's crazy!"

"Yes, I know," the manager said. "But now I want you to let him go."

"Let him go!" the fisherman cried, aghast. "You mustn't ever let this one go, Mr. Edwards! He's broke the record! He's the biggest turtle ever been caught on this island! Easy the biggest! And what about our money?"

"You'll get your money."

"I got the other five to pay off as well," the fisherman said, pointing down the beach.

About a hundred yards down, on the water's edge, five black-skinned almost naked men were standing beside a second boat. "All six of us are in on this, equal shares," the fisherman went on. "I can't let him go till we got the money."

"I guarantee you'll get it," the manager said. "Isn't that good enough for you?"

"I'll underwrite that guarantee," the father of the boy said, stepping forward. "And there'll be an extra bonus for all six of the fishermen just as long as you let him go at once. I mean immediately, this instant."

The fisherman looked at the father. Then he looked at the manager. "Okay," he said. "If that's the way you want it."

"There's one condition," the father said. "Before you

get your money, you must promise you won't go straight out and try to catch him again. Not this evening, anyway. Is that understood?"

"Sure," the fisherman said. "That's a deal." He turned and ran down the beach, calling to the other five fishermen. He shouted something to them that we couldn't hear, and in a minute or two, all six of them came back together. Five of them were carrying long thick wooden poles.

The boy was still kneeling beside the turtle's head. "David," the father said to him gently. "It's all right now, David. They're going to let him go."

The boy looked round, but he didn't take his arms from the turtle's neck, and he didn't get up. "When?" he asked.

"Now," the father said. "Right now. So you'd better come away."

"You promise?" the boy said.

"Yes, David, I promise."

The boy withdrew his arms. He got to his feet. He stepped back a few paces.

"Stand back, everyone!" shouted the fisherman called Willy. "Stand right back, everybody, please!"

The crowd moved a few yards up the beach. The tug-of-war men let go the rope and moved back with the others.

Willy got down on his hands and knees and crept very cautiously up to one side of the turtle. Then he began untying the knot in the rope. He kept well out of the range of the big flippers as he did this.

When the knot was untied, Willy crawled back. Then the five other fishermen stepped forward with their poles. The poles were about seven feet long and immensely thick. They wedged them underneath the shell of the turtle and began to rock the great creature from side to side on its shell. The shell had a high dome and was well shaped for rocking.

"Up and down!" sang the fishermen as they rocked away.

"Up and down! Up and down! Up and down!" The old turtle became thoroughly upset, and who could blame it? The big flippers lashed the air frantically, and the head kept shooting in and out of the shell.

"Roll him over!" sang the fishermen. "Up and over! Roll him over! One more time and over he goes!"

The turtle tilted high up onto its side and crashed down in the sand the right way up.

But it didn't walk away at once. The huge brown head came out and peered cautiously around.

"Go, turtle, go!" the small boy called out. "Go back to the sea!"

The two hooded black eyes of the turtle peered up at the boy. The eyes were bright and lively, full of the wisdom of great age. The boy looked back at the turtle, and this time when the boy spoke, his voice was soft and intimate. "Good-bye, old man," he said. "Go far away this time." The black eyes remained resting on the boy for a few seconds more. Nobody moved. Then, with great dignity, the massive beast turned away and began waddling toward the edge of the ocean. He didn't hurry. He moved sedately over the sandy beach, the big shell rocking gently from side to side as he went.

The crowd watched in silence.

He entered the water.

He kept going.

Soon he was swimming. He was in his element now. He swam gracefully and very fast, with the head held high. The sea was calm, and he made little waves that fanned out behind him on both sides, like the waves of a boat.

It was several minutes before we lost sight of him, and by then he was halfway to the horizon.

The guests began wandering back toward the hotel. They were curiously subdued. There was no joking or bantering now, no laughing. Something had happened. Something strange had come fluttering across the beach.

I walked back to my small balcony and sat down with a cigarette. I had an uneasy feeling that this was not the end of the affair.

The next morning at eight o'clock, the Jamaican girl, the one who had told me about Mr. Wasserman and the coconut, brought a glass of orange juice to my room.

"Big *big* fuss in the hotel this morning," she said as she placed the glass on the table and drew back the curtains. "Everyone flying about all over the place like they was crazy."

"Why? What's happened?"

"That little boy in number twelve, he's vanished. He disappeared in the night."

"You mean the turtle boy?"

"That's him," she said. "His parents is raising the roof and the manager's going mad."

"How long's he been missing?"

"About two hours ago his father found his bed empty. But he could've gone any time in the night I reckon."

"Yes," I said. "He could."

"Everybody in the hotel searching high and low," she said. "And a police car just arrived."

"Maybe he just got up early and went for a climb on the rocks," I said.

Her large, dark, haunted-looking eyes rested a moment on my face, then traveled away. "I do not think so," she said, and out she went.

I slipped on some clothes and hurried down to the beach. On the beach itself, two native policemen in khaki uniforms were standing with Mr. Edwards, the manager. Mr. Edwards was doing the talking. The policemen were listening patiently. In the distance, at both ends of the beach, I could see small groups of people, hotel servants as well as hotel guests, spreading out and heading for the rocks. The morning was beautiful. The sky was smoke blue, faintly glazed with yellow. The sun was up and making diamonds all over the smooth sea. And Mr. Edwards was talking loudly to the two native policemen, and waving his arms.

I wanted to help. What should I do? Which way should I go? It would be pointless simply to follow the others. So I just kept walking toward Mr. Edwards.

About then, I saw the fishing boat. The long wooden canoe with a single mast and a flapping brown sail was still some way out to sea, but it was heading for the beach. The two natives aboard, one at either end, were paddling hard. They were paddling very hard. The paddles rose and fell at such a terrific speed they might have been in a race. I stopped and watched them. Why the great rush to reach the shore? Quite obviously they had something to tell. I kept my eyes on the boat. Over to my left, I could hear Mr. Edwards saying to the two policemen, "It is perfectly ridiculous. I can't have people disappearing just like that from the hotel. You'd better find him fast, you understand me? He's either wandered off somewhere and got lost or he's been kidnapped. Either way, it's the responsibility of the police. . . ."

The fishing boat skimmed over the sea and came gliding up onto the sand at the water's edge. Both men dropped their paddles and jumped out. They started running up the beach. I recognized the one in front as Willy. When he caught sight of the manager and the two policemen, he made straight for them.

"Hey, Mr. Edwards!" Willy called out. "We just seen a crazy thing!"

The manager stiffened and jerked back his neck. The two policemen remained impassive. They were used to excitable people. They met them every day.

Willy stopped in front of the group, his chest heaving in

and out with heavy breathing. The other fisherman was close behind him. Their black skins were shining with sweat.

"We been paddling full speed for a long way," Willy said, excusing his out-of-breathness. "We thought we ought to come back and tell it as quick as we can."

"Tell what?" the manager said. "What did you see?"

"It was crazy man! Absolutely crazy!"

"Get on with it, Willy, for heaven's sake."

"You won't believe it," Willy said. "There ain't nobody going to believe it. Isn't that right, Tom?"

"That's right," the other fisherman said, nodding vigorously. "If Willy here hadn't been with me to prove it, I wouldn't have believed it myself!"

"Believed what?" Mr. Edwards said. "Just tell us what you saw."

"We'd gone off early," Willy said, "about four o'clock this morning, and we must've been a couple of miles out before it got light enough to see anything properly. Suddenly, as the sun comes up, we see right ahead of us, not more'n fifty yards away, we see something we couldn't believe not even with our own eyes. . . ."

"What?" snapped Mr. Edwards. "For heaven's sake, get on!"

"We sees that old monster turtle swimming away out there, the one on the beach yesterday, and we sees the boy sitting high up on the turtle's back and riding him over the sea like a horse!"

"You gotta believe it!" the other fisherman cried. "I sees it too, so you gotta believe it!"

Mr. Edwards looked at the two policemen. The two policemen looked at the fishermen. "You wouldn't be having us on, would you?" one of the policemen said.

"I swear it!" cried Willy. "It's the gospel truth! There's this tiny little boy riding high up on the old turtle's back and his feet isn't even touching the water! He's dry as a bone and sitting there comfy and easy as could be! So we go after them. Of course we go after them. At first we try creeping up on them very quietly, like we always do when we're catching a turtle, but the boy sees us. We aren't very far away at this time, you understand. No more than from here to the edge of the water. And when the boy sees us, he sort of leans forward as if he's saying something to that old turtle, and the turtle's head comes up and he starts swimming like the clappers of hell! Man, could that turtle go! Tom and me can paddle pretty quick when we want to, but we've no chance against that monster! No chance at all! He's going at least twice as fast as we are! Easy twice as fast, what you say, Tom?"

"I'd say he's going *three times* as fast," Tom said. "And I'll tell you why. In about ten or fifteen minutes, they're a mile ahead of us."

"Why on earth didn't you call out to the boy?" the manager asked. "Why didn't you speak to him earlier on, when you were closer?"

"We never *stop* calling out, man!" Willy cried. "As soon as the boy sees us and we're not trying to creep up on them any longer, then we start yelling. We yell everything under the sun at that boy to try and get him aboard. 'Hey boy!' I yell at him. 'You come on back with us! We'll give you a lift home! That ain't no good what you're doing there, boy! Jump off and swim while you got the chance and we'll pick you up! Go on, boy, jump! Your mammy must be waiting for you at home, boy, so why don't you come on in with us?' And once I shouted at him, 'Listen, boy! We're gonna make you a promise! We promise not to catch that old turtle if you come with us!' "

"Did he answer you at all?" the manager asked.

"He never even looks round!" Willy said. "He sits high

up on that shell and he's sort of rocking backward and forward with his body just like he's urging the old turtle to go faster and faster! You're gonna lose that little boy, Mr. Edwards, unless someone gets out there real quick and grabs him away!"

The manager's normally pink face had turned white as paper. "Which way were they heading?" he asked sharply.

"North," Willy answered. "Almost due north."

"Right!" the manager said. "We'll take the speedboat! I want you with us, Willy. And you, Tom."

The manager, the two policemen and the two fishermen ran down to where the boat that was used for water skiing lay beached on the sand. They pushed the boat out, and even the manager lent a hand, wading up to his knees in his well-pressed white trousers. Then they all climbed in.

I watched them go zooming off.

Two hours later, I watched them coming back. They had seen nothing.

All through that day, speedboats and yachts from other hotels along the coast searched the ocean. In the afternoon, the boy's father hired a helicopter. He rode in it himself, and they were up there three hours. They found no trace of the turtle or the boy.

For a week, the search went on, but with no result.

And now, nearly a year has gone by since it happened. In that time, there has been only one significant bit of news. A party of Americans, out from Nassau in the Bahamas, were deep-sea fishing off a large island called Eleuthera. There are literally thousands of coral reefs and small uninhabited islands in this area, and upon one of these tiny islands, the captain of the yacht saw through his binoculars the figure of a small person. There was a sandy beach on the island, and the small person was walking on the beach. The binoculars were passed around, and everyone who looked through them agreed that it was a child of some sort. There was, of course, a lot of excitement on board, and the fishing lines were quickly reeled in. The captain steered the yacht straight for the island. When they were half a mile off, they were able, through the binoculars, to see clearly that the figure on the beach was a boy, and although sun-burned, he was almost certainly white-skinned, not a native. At that point, the watchers on the yacht also spotted what looked like a giant turtle on the sand near the boy. What happened next, happened very quickly. The boy, who had probably caught sight of the approaching yacht, jumped onto the turtle's back, and the huge creature entered the water and swam at great speed around the island and out of sight. The yacht searched for two hours, but nothing more was seen either of the boy or the turtle.

There is no reason to disbelieve this report. There were five people on the yacht. Four of them were Americans and the captain was a Bahamian from Nassau. All of them in turn saw the boy and the turtle through the binoculars.

To reach Eleuthera Island from Jamaica by sea, one must first travel northeast for two hundred and fifty miles and pass through the Windward Passage between Cuba and Haiti. Then one must go north-northwest for a further three hundred miles at least. This is a total distance of five hundred and fifty miles, which is a very long journey for a small boy to make on the shell of a giant turtle.

Who knows what to think of all this?

One day, perhaps, he will come back, though I personally doubt it. I have a feeling he's quite happy where he is.

The Hitchhiker

I had a new car. It was an exciting toy, a big BMW 3.3 Li, which means 3.3 liter, long wheelbase, fuel injection. It had a top speed of 129 mph and terrific acceleration. The body was pale blue. The seats inside were darker blue and they were made of leather, genuine soft leather of the finest quality. The windows were electrically operated and so was the sunroof. The radio aerial popped up when I switched on the radio, and disappeared when I switched it off. The powerful engine growled and grunted impatiently at slow speeds, but at sixty miles an hour the growling stopped and the motor began to purr with pleasure.

I was driving up to London by myself. It was a lovely June day. They were haymaking in the fields and there were buttercups along both sides of the road. I was whispering along at 70 mph, leaning back comfortably in my seat, with no more than a couple of fingers resting lightly on the wheel to keep her steady. Ahead of me I saw a man thumbing a lift. I touched the brake and brought the car to a stop beside him. I always stopped for hitchhikers. I knew just how it used to feel to be standing on the side of a country road watching the cars go by. I hated the drivers for pretending they didn't see me, especially the ones in big cars with three empty seats. The large expensive cars seldom stopped. It was always the smaller ones that offered you a lift, or the old rusty ones or the ones that were already crammed full of children and the driver would say, "I think we can squeeze in one more."

The hitchhiker poked his head through the open window

and said, "Going to London, guv'nor?"

"Yes," I said. "Jump in."

He got in and I drove on.

He was a small ratty-faced man with gray teeth. His eyes were dark and quick and clever, like rat's eyes, and his ears were slightly pointed at the top. He had a cloth cap on his head and he was wearing a grayish-colored jacket with enormous pockets. The gray jacket, together with the quick eyes and the pointed ears, made him look more than anything like some sort of a huge human rat.

"What part of London are you headed for?" I asked him.

"I'm goin' right through London and out the other side," he said. "I'm goin' to Epsom, for the races. It's Derby Day today."

"So it is," I said. "I wish I were going with you. I love betting on horses."

"I never bet on horses," he said. "I don't even watch 'em run. That's a stupid silly business."

"Then why do you go?" I asked.

He didn't seem to like that question. His little ratty face went absolutely blank and he sat there staring straight ahead at the road, saying nothing.

"I expect you help to work the betting machines or something like that," I said.

"That's even sillier," he answered. "There's no fun working them lousy machines and selling tickets to mugs. Any fool could do that."

There was a long silence. I decided not to question him any more. I remembered how irritated I used to get in my hitchhiking days when drivers kept asking *me* questions. Where are you going? Why are you going there? What's your job? Are you married? Do you have a girl friend? What's her name? How old are you? And so forth and so forth. I used to hate it.

"I'm sorry," I said. "It's none of my business what you do. The trouble is, I'm a writer, and most writers are terribly nosy."

"You write books?" he asked.

"Yes."

"Writin' books is okay," he said. "It's what I call a skilled trade. I'm in a skilled trade too. The folks I despise is them that spend all their lives doin' crummy old routine jobs with no skill in 'em at all. You see what I mean?"

"Yes."

"The secret of life," he said, "is to become very very good at somethin' that's very very 'ard to do."

"Like you," I said.

"Exactly. You and me both."

"What makes you think that *I'm* any good at my job?" I asked. "There's an awful lot of bad writers around."

"You wouldn't be drivin' about in a car like this if you weren't no good at it," he answered. It must've cost a tidy packet, this little job."

"It wasn't cheap."

"What can she do flat out?" he asked.

"One hundred and twenty-nine miles an hour," I told him.

"I'll bet she won't do it."

"I'll bet she will."

"All car-makers is liars," he said. "You can buy any car you like and it'll never do what the makers say it will in the ads."

"This one will."

"Open 'er up then and prove it," he said. "Go on, guv'nor, open 'er right up and let's see what she'll do."

There is a traffic circle at Chalfont St. Peter and immediately beyond it there's a long straight section of divided highway. We came out of the circle onto the highway and I pressed my foot hard down on the accelerator. The big car leaped forward as though she'd been stung. In ten seconds or so, we were doing ninety.

"Lovely!" he cried. "Beautiful! Keep goin'!"

I had the accelerator jammed right down against the floor and I held it there.

"One hundred!" he shouted. "A hundred and five! A hundred and ten! A hundred and fifteen! Go on! Don't slack off!"

I was in the outside lane and we flashed past several cars as though they were standing still—a green Mini, a big cream-colored Citroen, a white Land Rover, a huge truck with a container on the back, an orange-colored Volkswagen Minibus. . . .

"A hundred and twenty!" my passenger shouted, jumping up and down. "Go on! Go on! Get 'er up to one-two-nine!"

At that moment, I heard the scream of a police siren. It was so loud it seemed to be right inside the car, and then a cop on a motorcycle loomed up alongside us on the inside lane and went past us and raised a hand for us to stop.

"Oh, my sainted aunt!" I said. "That's torn it!"

The cop must have been doing about a hundred and thirty when he passed us, and he took plenty of time slowing down. Finally, he pulled to the side of the road and I pulled in behind him. "I didn't know police motorcycles could go as fast as that," I said rather lamely.

"That one can," my passenger said. "It's the same make as yours. It's a BMW R90S. Fastest bike on the road. That's what they're usin' nowadays."

The cop got off his motorcycle and leaned the machine sideways onto its prop stand. Then he took off his gloves and placed them carefully on the seat. He was in no hurry now. He had us where he wanted us and he knew it.

"This is real trouble," I said. "I don't like it one little bit."

"Don't talk to 'im more than is necessary, you understand," my companion said. "Just sit tight and keep mum."

Like an executioner approaching his victim, the cop came strolling slowly toward us. He was a big meaty man with a belly, and his blue breeches were skin-tight around his enormous thighs. His goggles were pulled up onto the helmet, showing a smoldering red face with wide cheeks.

We sat there like guilty schoolboys, waiting for him to arrive.

"Watch out for this man," my passenger whispered, " 'e looks mean as the devil."

The cop came around to my open window and placed one meaty hand on the sill. "What's the hurry?" he said.

"No hurry, officer," I answered.

"Perhaps there's a woman in the back having a baby and you're rushing her to hospital? Is that it?"

"No, officer."

"Or perhaps your house is on fire and you're dashing home to rescue the family from upstairs?" His voice was dangerously soft and mocking.

"My house isn't on fire, officer."

"In that case," he said, "you've got yourself into a nasty mess, haven't you? Do you know what the speed limit is in this country?"

"Seventy," I said.

"And do you mind telling me exactly what speed you were doing just now?"

I shrugged and didn't say anything.

When he spoke next, he raised his voice so loud that I jumped. *"One hundred and twenty miles per hour!"* he barked. "That's *fifty* miles an hour over the limit!"

He turned his head and spat out a big gob of spit. It landed on the wing of my car and started sliding down over my beautiful blue paint. Then he turned back again and stared hard at my passenger. "And who are you?" he asked sharply.

"He's a hitchhiker," I said. "I'm giving him a lift."

"I didn't ask you," he said. "I asked him."

" 'Ave I done somethin' wrong?" my passenger asked. His voice was soft and oily as haircream.

"That's more than likely," the cop answered. "Anyway, you're a witness. I'll deal with you in a minute. Driver's license," he snapped, holding out his hand.

I gave him my driver's license.

He unbuttoned the left-hand breast pocket of his tunic and brought out the dreaded book of tickets. Carefully, he copied the name and address from my license. Then he gave it back to me. He strolled around to the front of the car and read the number from the license plate and wrote that down as well. He filled in the date, the time and the details of my offense. Then he tore out the top copy of the ticket. But before handing it to me, he checked that all the information had come through clearly on his own carbon copy. Finally, he replaced the book in his breast pocket and fastened the button.

"Now you," he said to my passenger, and he walked around to the other side of the car. From the other breast pocket he produced a small black notebook. "Name?" he snapped.

"Michael Fish," my passenger said.

"Address?"

"Fourteen, Windsor Lane, Luton."

"Show me something to prove this is your real name and address," the policeman said.

My passenger fished in his pockets and came out with a driver's license of his own. The policeman checked the name and address and handed it back to him. "What's your job?" he asked sharply.

"I'm an 'od carrier."

"A *what?*"

"An 'od carrier."

"Spell it."

"H-o-d c-a—"

"That'll do. And what's a hod carrier, may I ask?"

"An 'od carrier, officer, is a person 'oo carries the cement up the ladder to the bricklayer. And the 'od is what 'ee carries it in. It's got a long 'andle, and on the top you've got bits of wood set at an angle . . ."

"All right, all right. Who's your employer?"

"Don't 'ave one. I'm unemployed."

The cop wrote all this down in the black notebook. Then he returned the book to its pocket and did up the button.

"When I get back to the station I'm going to do a little checking up on you," he said to my passenger.

"Me? What've I done wrong?" the rat-faced man asked.

"I don't like your face, that's all," the cop said. "And we just might have a picture of it somewhere in our files." He strolled round the car and returned to my window.

"I suppose you know you're in serious trouble," he said to me.

"Yes, officer."

"You won't be driving this fancy car of yours again for a very long time, not after *we've* finished with you. You won't be driving *any* car again, come to that, for several years. And a good thing, too. I hope they lock you up for a spell into the bargain."

"You mean prison?" I asked, alarmed.

"Absolutely," he said, smacking his lips. "In the clink. Behind the bars. Along with all the other criminals who break the law. *And* a hefty fine into the bargain. Nobody will be more pleased about that than me. I'll see you in court, both of you. You'll be getting a summons to appear."

He turned away and walked over to his motorcycle. He flipped the prop stand back into position with his foot and

swung his leg over the saddle. Then he kicked the starter
and roared off up the road out of sight.

"Phew!" I gasped. "That's done it."

"We was caught," my passenger said. "We was caught
good and proper."

"I was caught, you mean."

"That's right," he said. "What you goin' to do now, guv'-
nor?"

"I'm going straight up to London to talk to my solicitor,"
I said. I started the car and drove on.

"You mustn't believe what 'ee said to you about goin' to
prison," my passenger said. "They don't put nobody in the
clink just for speedin'."

"Are you sure of that?" I asked.

"I'm positive," he answered. "They can take your license
away and they can give you a whoppin' big fine, but that'll
be the end of it."

I felt tremendously relieved.

"By the way," I said, "why did you lie to him?"

"Who, me?" he said. "What makes you think I lied?"

"You told him you were an unemployed hod carrier. But
you told *me* you were in a highly skilled trade."

"So I am," he said. "But it don't pay to tell everythin' to
a copper."

"So what *do* you do?" I asked him.

"Ah," he said slyly. "That'd be tellin', wouldn't it?"

"Is it something you're ashamed of?"

"Ashamed?" he cried. "Me, ashamed of my job? I'm about
as proud of it as anybody could be in the entire world!"

"Then why won't you tell me?"

"You writers really is nosy parkers, aren't you?" he said.
"And you ain't goin' to be 'appy, I don't think, until you've
found out exactly what the answer is?"

"I don't really care one way or the other," I told him,
lying.

He gave me a crafty little ratty look out of the sides of
his eyes. "I think you do care," he said. "I can see it on your
face that you think I'm in some kind of a very peculiar trade
and you're just achin' to know what it is."

I didn't like the way he read my thoughts. I kept quiet and
stared at the road ahead.

"You'd be right, too," he went on. "I *am* in a very peculiar
trade. I'm in the queerest peculiar trade of 'em all."

I waited for him to go on.

"That's why I 'as to be extra careful oo' I'm talkin' to,
you see. 'Ow am I to know, for instance, you're not another
copper in plain clothes?"

"Do I look like a copper?"

"No," he said. "You don't. And you ain't. Any fool could
tell that."

He took from his pocket a tin of tobacco and a packet of
cigarette papers and started to roll a cigarette. I was watching him out of the corner of one eye, and the speed with
which he performed this rather difficult operation was incredible. The cigarette was rolled and ready in about five seconds. He ran his tongue along the edge of the paper, stuck
it down and popped the cigarette between his lips. Then, as
if from nowhere, a lighter appeared in his hand. The lighter
flamed. The cigarette was lit. The lighter disappeared. It
was altogether a remarkable performance.

"I've never seen anyone roll a cigarette as fast as that,"
I said.

"Ah," he said, taking a deep suck of smoke. "So you
noticed."

"Of course I noticed. It was quite fantastic."

He sat back and smiled. It pleased him very much that I
had noticed how quickly he could roll a cigarette. "You want
to know what makes me able to do it?" he asked.

"Go on then."

"It's because I've got fantastic fingers. These fingers of

mine," he said, holding up both hands high in front of him, "are quicker and cleverer than the fingers of the best piano player in the world!"

"Are you a piano player?"

"Don't be daft," he said. "Do I look like a piano player?"

I glanced at his fingers. They were so beautifully shaped, so slim and long and elegant, they didn't seem to belong to the rest of him at all. They looked more like the fingers of a brain surgeon or a watchmaker.

"My job," he went on, "is a hundred times more difficult than playin' the piano. Any twerp can learn to do that. There's titchy little kids learnin' to play the piano in almost any 'ouse you go into these days. That's right, ain't it?"

"More or less," I said.

"Of course it's right. But there's not one person in ten million can learn to do what I do. Not one in ten million! 'Ow about that?"

"Amazing," I said.

"You're darn right it's amazin'," he said.

"I think I know what you do," I said. "You do conjuring tricks. You're a conjuror."

"Me?" he snorted. "A conjuror? Can you picture me goin' round crummy kid's parties makin' rabbits come out of top 'ats?"

"Then you're a card player. You get people into card games and you deal yourself marvelous hands."

"Me! A rotten cardsharper!" he cried. "That's a miserable racket if ever there was one."

"All right. I give up."

I was taking the car along slowly now, at no more than forty miles an hour, to make quite sure I wasn't stopped again. We had come onto the main London-Oxford road and were running down the hill toward Denham.

Suddenly, my passenger was holding up a black leather

belt in his hand. "Ever seen this before?" he asked. The belt had a brass buckle of unusual design.

"Hey!" I said. "That's mine, isn't it? It *is* mine! Where did you get it?"

He grinned and waved the belt gently from side to side. "Where d'you think I got it?" he said. "Off the top of your trousers, of course."

I reached down and felt for my belt. It was gone.

"You mean you took it off me while we've been driving along?" I asked flabbergasted.

He nodded, watching me all the time with those little black ratty eyes.

"That's impossible," I said. "You'd have had to undo the buckle and slide the whole thing out through the loops all the way round. I'd have seen you doing it. And even if I hadn't seen you, I'd have felt it."

"Ah, but you didn't, did you?" he said, triumphant. He dropped the belt on his lap, and now all at once there was a brown shoelace dangling from his fingers. "And what about this, then?" he exclaimed, waving the shoelace.

"What about it?" I said.

"Anyone around 'ere missin' a shoelace?" he asked, grinning.

I glanced down at my shoes. The lace of one of them was missing. "Good grief!" I said. "How did you do that? I never saw you bending down."

"You never saw nothin'," he said proudly. "You never even saw me move an inch. And you know why?"

"Yes," I said. "Because you've got fantastic fingers."

"Exactly right!" he cried. "You catch on pretty quick, don't you?" He sat back and sucked away at his homemade cigarette, blowing the smoke out in a thin stream against the windshield. He knew he had impressed me greatly with those two tricks, and this made him very happy. "I don't want to be late," he said. "What time is it?"

"There's a clock in front of you," I told him.

"I don't trust car clocks," he said. "What does your watch say?"

I hitched up my sleeve to look at the watch on my wrist. It wasn't there. I looked at the man. He looked back at me, grinning.

"You've taken that, too," I said.

He held out his hand and there was my watch lying in his palm. "Nice bit of stuff, this," he said. "Superior quality. Eighteen-carat gold. Easy to sell, too. It's never any trouble gettin' rid of quality goods."

"I'd like it back, if you don't mind," I said rather huffily.

He placed the watch carefully on the leather tray in front of him. "I wouldn't nick anything from you, guv'nor," he said. "You're my pal. You're givin' me a lift."

"I'm glad to hear it," I said.

"All I'm doin' is answerin' your question," he went on. "You asked me what I did for a livin' and I'm showin' you."

"What else have you got of mine?"

He smiled again, and now he started to take from the pocket of his jacket one thing after another that belonged to me—my driver's license, a key ring with four keys on it, some pound notes, a few coins, a letter from my publishers, my diary, a stubby old pencil, a cigarette lighter, and last of all, a beautiful old sapphire ring with pearls around it belonging to my wife. I was taking the ring up to a jeweler in London because one of the pearls was missing.

"Now *there's* another lovely piece of goods," he said, turning the ring over in his fingers. "That's eighteenth century, if I'm not mistaken, from the reign of King George the Third."

"You're right," I said, impressed. "You're absolutely right."

He put the ring on the leather tray with the other items.

"So you're a pickpocket," I said.

"I don't like that word," he answered. "It's a coarse and vulgar word. Pickpockets is coarse and vulgar people who only do easy little amateur jobs. They lift money from blind old ladies."

"What do you call yourself, then?"

"Me? I'm a fingersmith. I'm a professional fingersmith." He spoke the words solemnly and proudly, as though he were telling me he was the President of the Royal College of Surgeons or the Archbishop of Cantebury.

"I've never heard that word before," I said. "Did you invent it?"

"Of course I didn't invent it," he replied. "It's the name given to them who's risen to the very top of the profession. You've 'eard of a goldsmith and a silversmith, for instance. They're experts with gold and silver. I'm an expert with my fingers, so I'm a fingersmith."

"It must be an interesting job."

"It's a marvelous job," he answered. "It's lovely."

"And that's why you go to the races?"

"Race meetings is easy meat," he said. "You just stand around after the race, watchin' for the lucky ones to queue up and draw their money. And when you see someone collectin' a big bundle of notes, you simply follows after 'im and 'elps yourself. But don't get me wrong, guv'nor. I never takes nothin' from a loser. Nor from poor people neither. I only go after them as can afford it, the winners and the rich."

"That's very thoughtful of you," I said. "How often do you get caught?"

"Caught?" he cried, disgusted. "*Me* get caught! It's only pickpockets get caught. Fingersmiths never. Listen, I could take the false teeth out of your mouth if I wanted to and you wouldn't even catch me!"

"I don't have false teeth," I said.

"I know you don't," he answered. "Otherwise I'd 'ave 'ad
'em out long ago!"

I believed him. Those long slim fingers of his seemed able
to do anything.

We drove on for a while without talking.

"That policeman's going to check up on you pretty thoroughly," I said. "Doesn't that worry you a bit?"

"Nobody's checkin' up on me," he said.

"Of course they are. He's got your name and address
written down most carefully in his black book."

The man gave me another of his sly ratty little smiles.
"Ah," he said. "So 'ee 'as. But I'll bet 'ee ain't got it all
written down in 'is memory as well. I've never known a
copper yet with a decent memory. Some of 'em can't even
remember their own names."

"What's memory got to do with it?" I asked. "It's written
down in his book, isn't it?"

"Yes, guv'nor, it is. But the trouble is, 'ee's lost the book.
'Ee's lost both books, the one with my name in it *and* the one
with yours."

In the long delicate fingers of his right hand, the man
was holding up in triumph the two books he had taken from
the policeman's pockets. "Easiest job I ever done," he announced proudly.

I nearly swerved the car into a milk truck, I was so
excited.

"That copper's got nothin' on either of us now," he said.

"You're a genius!" I cried.

" 'Ee's got no names, no addresses, no car number, no
nothin'," he said.

"You're brilliant!"

"I think you'd better pull in off this main road as soon as

possible," he said. "Then we'd better build a little bonfire and burn these books."

"You're a fantastic fellow!" I exclaimed.

"Thank you, guv'nor," he said. "It's always nice to be appreciated."

The Mildenhall Treasure

A NOTE ABOUT THE NEXT STORY

In 1946, more than thirty years ago, I was still unmarried and living with my mother. I was making a fair income by writing two short stories a year. Each of them took four months to complete, and fortunately there were people both at home and abroad who were willing to buy them.

One morning in April of that year, I read in the newspaper about a remarkable find of Roman silver. It had been discovered three years before by a plowman near Mildenhall, in the county of Suffolk, but the discovery had for some reason been kept secret until then. The newspaper article said it was the greatest treasure ever found in the British Isles, and it had now been acquired by the British Museum. The name of the plowman was given as Gordon Butcher.

True stories about the finding of really big treasure send shivers of electricity all the way down my legs to the soles of my feet. The moment I read that story, I leaped up from my chair without finishing my breakfast and shouted goodbye to my mother and rushed out to my car. The car was a nine-year-old Wolseley, and I called it "The Hard Black Slinker." It went well but not very fast.

Mildenhall was about one hundred twenty miles from my home, a tricky cross-country trip along twisty roads and country lanes. I got there at lunchtime, and by asking at the local police station, I found the small house where Gordon Butcher lived with his family. He was at home having his lunch when I knocked on his door.

I asked him if he would mind talking to me about how he found the treasure.

"No, thank you," he said. "I've had enough of reporters. I don't want to see another reporter for the rest of my life."

"I'm not a reporter," I told him. "I'm a short-story writer and I sell my work to magazines. They pay good money." I went on to say that if he would tell me exactly how he found the treasure, then I would write a truthful story about it. And if I was lucky enough to sell it, I would split the money equally with him.

In the end, he agreed to talk to me. We sat for several hours in his little kitchen, and he told me an enthralling story. When he had finished, I paid a visit to the other man in the affair, an older fellow called Ford. Ford wouldn't talk to me and closed the door in my face. But by then I had my story and I set out for home.

The next morning, I went up to the British Museum in London to see the treasure that Gordon Butcher had found. It was fabulous. I got the shivers all over again just from looking at it.

I wrote the story as truthfully as I possibly could and sent it off to America. It was bought by the *Saturday Evening Post,* and I was well paid. When the money arrived, I sent exactly half of it to Gordon Butcher in Mildenhall.

One week later, I received a letter from Mr. Butcher written upon what must have been a page torn from a child's school exercise book. It said in part, "... you could have knocked me over with a feather when I saw your cheque. It was lovely. I want to thank you. ..."

Here is the story almost exactly as it was written thirty years ago. I've changed it very little. I've simply toned down some of the more flowery passages and taken out a number of superfluous adjectives and unnecessary sentences.

Around seven o'clock in the morning, Gordon Butcher got out of bed and switched on the light. He walked barefoot to the window and drew back the curtains and looked out.

This was January so it was still dark, but he could tell there hadn't been any snow in the night.

"That wind," he said aloud to his wife. "Just listen to that wind."

His wife was out of bed now, standing beside him near the window, and the two of them were silent, listening to the swish and whisk of the icy wind as it came sweeping in over the fens.

"It's a nor'easter," he said.

"There'll be snow for certain before nightfall," she told him. "And plenty of it."

She was dressed before him, and she went into the next room and leaned over the cot of her six-year-old daughter and gave her a kiss. She called out a good morning to the two older children in the third room, then she went downstairs to make breakfast.

At a quarter to eight, Gordon Butcher put on his coat, his cap and his leather gloves and walked out the back door into the bitter early-morning winter weather. As he moved through the half-daylight over the yard to the shed where his bicycle stood, the wind was like a knife on his cheek. He wheeled out the bike and mounted and began to ride down the middle of the narrow road, right into the face of the gale.

Gordon Butcher was thirty-eight. He was not an ordinary

farm laborer. He took orders from no man unless he wished. He owned his own tractor, and with this he plowed other men's fields and gathered other men's harvests under contract. His thoughts were only for his wife, his son, his two daughters. His wealth was in his small brick house, his two cows, his tractor, his skill as a plowman.

Gordon Butcher's head was very curiously shaped, the back of it protruding like the sharp end of an enormous egg, and his ears stuck out, and a front tooth was missing on the left side. But none of this seemed to matter very much when you met him face to face in the open air. He looked at you with steady blue eyes that were without any malice or cunning or greed. And the mouth didn't have those thin lines of bitterness around the edges that one so often sees on men who work the land and spend their days fighting the weather.

His only eccentricity, to which he would cheerfully admit if you asked him, was talking aloud to himself when he was alone. This habit, he said, grew from the fact that the kind of work he did left him entirely by himself for ten hours a day, six days a week. "It keeps me company," he said, "hearing me own voice now and again."

He biked on down the road, pedaling hard against the brutal wind.

"All right," he said, "all right, why don't you blow a bit? Is that the best you can do? My goodness me, I hardly know you're there this morning!" The wind howled around him and snapped at his coat and squeezed its way through the pores of the heavy wool, through his jacket underneath, through his shirt and vest, and it touched his bare skin with an icy fingertip. "Why," he said, "it's lukewarm you are today. You'll have to do a sight better than that if you're going to make *me* shiver."

And now the darkness was diluting into a pale gray

morning light, and Gordon Butcher could see the cloudy roof
of the sky very low above his head and flying with the
wind. Gray blue the clouds were, flecked here and there with
black, a solid mass from horizon to horizon, the whole thing
moving with the wind, sliding past above his head like a
great gray sheet of metal unrolling. All around him lay the
bleak and lonely fen country of Suffolk, mile upon mile of
it that went on for ever.

He pedaled on. He rode through the outskirts of the little
town of Mildenhall and headed for the village of West Row,
where the man called Ford had his place.

He had left his tractor at Ford's the day before because
his next job was to plow up four and a half acres on Thistley Green for Ford. It was not Ford's land; it is important
to remember this. But Ford was the one who had asked him
to do the work.

Actually a farmer called Rolfe owned the four and a half
acres.

Rolfe had asked Ford to get it plowed because Ford, like
Gordon Butcher, did plowing jobs for other men. The difference between Ford and Gordon Butcher was that Ford
was somewhat grander. He was a fairly prosperous small-
time agricultural engineer who had a nice house and a
large yard full of sheds filled with farm implements and
machinery. Gordon Butcher had only his one tractor.

On this occasion, however, when Rolfe had asked Ford
to plow up his four and a half acres on Thistley Green, Ford
was too busy to do the work so he hired Gordon Butcher
to do it for him.

There was no one about in Ford's yard when Butcher
rode in. He parked his bike, filled up his tractor with paraffin and gasoline, warmed the engine, hitched the plow behind, mounted the high seat and drove out to Thistley
Green.

The field was not half a mile away, and around eight-thirty Butcher drove the tractor in through the gate onto the field itself. Thistley Green was maybe a hundred acres all told, with a low hedge running round it. And although it was actually one large field, different parts of it were owned by different men. These separate parts were easy to define because each was cultivated in its own way. Rolfe's plot of four and a half acres was over to one side near the southern boundary fence. Butcher knew where it was and drove his tractor round the edge of the field, then inward until he was on the plot.

The plot was barley stubble now, covered with the short and rotting yellow stalks of barley harvested last fall, and only recently it had been broad-sheared so that now it was ready for the plow.

"Deep-plow it," Ford had said to Butcher the day before. "It's for sugar beet. Rolfe's putting sugar beet in there."

They only plow about four inches down for barley, but for sugar beet they plow deep, to ten or twelve inches. A horse-drawn plow can't plow as deep as that. It was only since tractors came along that the farmers had been able to deep-plow properly. Rolfe's land had been deep-plowed for sugar beet some years before this, but it wasn't Butcher who had done the plowing and no doubt the job had been skimped a bit and the plowman had not gone quite as deep as he should. Had he done so, what was about to happen today would probably have happened then, and that would have been a different story.

Gordon Butcher began to plow. Up and down the field he went, lowering the plow deeper and deeper each trip until at last it was cutting twelve inches into the ground and turning up a smooth, even wave of black earth as it went.

The wind was coming faster now, rushing in from the killer sea, sweeping over the flat Norfolk fields, past Saxthorpe and Reepham and Honingham and Swaffham and

Larling and over the border to Suffolk, to Mildenhall and to Thistley Green where Gordon Butcher sat upright high on the seat of his tractor, driving back and forth over the plot of yellow barley stubble that belonged to Rolfe. Gordon Butcher could smell the sharp crisp smell of snow not far away; he could see the low roof of the sky, no longer flecked with black, but pale and whitish gray sliding by overhead like a solid sheet of metal unrolling.

"Well," he said, raising his voice above the clatter of the tractor, "you are surely angry at somebody today. What an almighty fuss it is now of blowin' and whistlin' and freezin'. Like a woman," he added. "Just like a woman does sometimes in the evening." And he kept his eye upon the line of the furrow, and he smiled.

At noon he stopped the tractor, dismounted and fished in his pocket for his lunch. He found it and sat on the ground in the lee of one of the huge tractor wheels. He ate large pieces of bread and very small pieces of cheese. He had nothing to drink, for his only Thermos had got smashed by the jolting of the tractor two weeks before, and in wartime, for this was in January 1942, you could not buy another anywhere. For about fifteen minutes he sat on the ground in the shelter of the wheel and ate his lunch. Then he got up and examined his peg.

Unlike many plowmen, Butcher always hitched his plow to the tractor with a wooden peg so that if the plow fouled a root or a large stone, the peg would simply break at once, leaving the plow behind and saving the plowshares from serious damage. All over the black fen country, just below the surface, lie enormous trunks of ancient oak trees, and a wooden peg will save a plowshare many times a week out there. Although Thistley Green was well-cultivated land— field land, not fen land—Butcher was taking no chances with his plow.

He examined the wooden peg, found it sound, mounted

the tractor again and went on with his plowing.

The tractor nosed back and forth over the ground, leaving a smooth brown wave of soil behind it. And still the wind blew colder, but it did not snow.

Around three o'clock the thing happened.

There was a slight jolt, the wooden peg broke, and the tractor left the plow behind. Butcher stopped, dismounted and walked back to the plow to see what it had struck. It was surprising for this to have happened here, on field land. There should be no oak trees underneath the soil in this place.

He knelt down beside the plow and began to scoop the soil away around the point of the plowshare. The lower tip of the share was twelve inches down. There was a lot of soil to be scooped up. He dug his gloved fingers into the earth and scooped it out with both hands. Six inches down ... eight inches ... ten inches ... twelve. He slid his fingers along the blade of the plowshare until they reached the forward point of it. The soil was loose and crumbly, and it kept falling back into the hole he was digging. He could not therefore see the twelve-inch-deep point of the share. He could only feel it. And now he could feel that the point was indeed lodged against something solid. He scooped away more earth. He enlarged the hole. It was necessary to see clearly what sort of an obstacle he had struck. If it was fairly small, then perhaps he could dig it out with his hands and get on with the job. If it was a tree trunk, he would have to go back to Ford's and fetch a spade.

"Come on," he said aloud. "I'll have you out of there, you hidden demon, you rotten old thing." And suddenly, as the gloved fingers scraped away a final handful of black earth, he caught sight of the curved rim of something flat, like the rim of a huge thick plate, sticking up out of the soil. He rubbed the rim with his fingers, and he rubbed again. Then all at once, the rim gave off a greenish glint, and Gordon Butcher bent his head closer and closer still, peering down into the little hole he had dug with his hands. For one last time, he rubbed the rim clean with his fingers, and in a flash of light, he saw clearly the unmistakable blue-green crust of ancient buried metal, and his heart stood still.

It should be explained here that farmers in this part of Suffolk, and particularly in the Mildenhall area, have for years been turning up ancient objects from the soil. Flint arrowheads from very long ago have been found in considerable numbers, but more interesting than that, Roman pottery and Roman implements have also been found. It is known that the Romans favored this part of the country during their occupation of Britain, and all local farmers are therefore well aware of the possibility of finding something interesting during a day's work. And so there was a kind of permanent awareness among Mildenhall people of the presence of treasure underneath the earth of their land.

Gordon Butcher's reaction, as soon as he saw the rim of that enormous plate, was a curious one. He immediately drew away. Then he got to his feet and turned his back on what he had just seen. He paused only long enough to switch off the engine of his tractor before he walked off fast in the direction of the road.

He did not know precisely what impulse caused him to stop digging and walk away. He will tell you that the only thing he can remember about those first few seconds was the whiff of danger that came to him from that little patch of greenish blue. The moment he touched it with his fingers, something electric went through his body, and there came to him a powerful premonition that this was a thing that could destroy the peace and happiness of many people.

In the beginning, all he had wished was to be away from it, to leave it behind him and be done with it forever. But after he had gone a hundred yards or so, he began to slow his pace. At the gate leading out from Thistley Green, he stopped.

"What in the world is the matter with you, Mr. Gordon Butcher?" he said aloud to the howling wind. "Are you frightened or something? No, I'm not frightened. But I'll tell you straight, I'm not keen to handle this alone."

That was when he thought of Ford.

He thought of Ford at first because it was for him that he was working. He thought of him second because he knew that Ford was a kind of collector of old stuff, of all the old stones and arrowheads that people kept digging up from time to time in the district, which they brought to Ford and which Ford placed upon the mantel in his parlor. It was believed that Ford sold these things, but no one knew or cared how he did it.

Gordon Butcher turned toward Ford's place and walked fast out of the gate onto the narrow road, down the road around the sharp left-hand corner and so to the house. He found Ford in his large shed bending over a damaged harrow, mending it. Butcher stood by the door and said, "Mr. Ford!"

Ford looked around without straightening his body.

"Well, Gordon," he said, "what is it?"

Ford was middle-aged or a little older, bald-headed, long-nosed, with a clever foxy look about his face. His mouth was thin and sour, and when he looked at you, and when you saw the tightness of his mouth and the thin sour line of his lips, you knew that this was a mouth that never smiled. His chin receded, his nose was long and sharp and he had the air about him of a sour old crafty fox from the woods.

"What is it?" he said, looking up from the harrow.

Gordon Butcher stood by the door, blue-cheeked with cold, a little out of breath, rubbing his hands slowly one against the other.

"The tractor left the plow behind," he said quietly. "There's metal down there. I saw it."

Ford's head gave a jerk. "What kind of metal?" he said sharply.

"Flat. Quite flat like a sort of huge plate."

"You didn't dig it out?" Ford had straightened up now and there was a glint of eagles in his eyes.

Butcher said, "No, I left it alone and came straight on here."

Ford walked quickly over to the corner and took his coat off the nail. He found a cap and gloves, then he found a spade and went toward the door. There was something odd, he noticed, in Butcher's manner.

"You're sure it was metal?"

"Crusted up," Butcher said. "But it was metal all right."

"How deep?"

"Twelve inches down. At least the top of it was twelve inches down. The rest is deeper."

"How d'you know it was a plate?"

"I don't," Butcher said. "I only saw a little bit of the rim. But it looked like a plate to me. An enormous plate."

Ford's foxy face went quite white with excitement. "Come on," he said. "We'll go back and see."

The two men walked out of the shed into the fierce, ever-mounting fury of the wind. Ford shivered.

"Curse this filthy weather," he said. "Curse and blast this filthy freezing weather," and he sank his pointed foxy face deep into the collar of his coat and began to ponder upon the possibilities of Butcher's find.

One thing Ford knew that Butcher did not know. He knew that back in 1932 a man called Lethbridge, a lecturer in Anglo-Saxon antiquities at Cambridge University, had been excavating in the district and that he had actually unearthed the foundations of a Roman villa on Thistley Green itself. Ford was not forgetting that, and he quickened his pace.

Butcher walked beside him without speaking, and soon they were there. They went through the gate and over the field to the plow, which lay about ten yards behind the tractor.

Ford knelt down beside the front of the plow and peered into the small hole Gordon Butcher had dug with his hands. He touched the rim of green-blue metal with a gloved finger. He scraped away a bit more earth. He leaned farther forward so that his pointed nose was right down the hole. He ran his fingers over the rough green surface. Then he stood up and said, "Let's get the plow out of the way and do some digging." Although there were fireworks exploding in his head and shivers running all over his body, Ford kept his voice very soft and casual.

Between them they pulled the plow back a couple of yards.

"Give me the spade," Ford said, and he began cautiously to dig the soil away in a circle about three feet in diameter around the exposed patch of metal. When the hole was two feet deep, he threw away the spade and used his hands. He knelt down and scraped the soil away, and gradually the little patch of metal grew and grew until at last there lay exposed before them the great round disk of an enormous plate. It was fully twenty-four inches in diameter. The lower point of the plow had just caught the raised center rim of the plate, for one could see the dent.

Carefully Ford lifted it out of the hole. He got to his feet and stood wiping the soil away from it, turning it over and over in his hands. There was nothing much to see, for the whole surface was crusted over with a thick layer of a hard greenish-blue substance. But he knew that it was an enormous plate or dish of great weight and thickness. It weighed about eighteen pounds!

Ford stood in the field of yellow barley stubble and gazed at the huge plate. His hands began to shake. A tremendous and almost unbearable excitement started boiling up inside him, and it was not easy for him to hide it. But he did his best.

"Some sort of a dish," he said.

Butcher was kneeling on the ground beside the hole. "Must be pretty old," he said.

"Could be old," Ford said. "But it's all rusted up and eaten away."

"That don't look like rust to me," Butcher said. "That greenish stuff isn't rust. It's something else."

"It's green rust," Ford said rather superbly, and that ended the discussion.

Butcher, still on his knees, was poking about casually in the now three-foot-wide hole with his gloved hands. "There's another one down here," he said.

Instantly, Ford laid the great dish on the ground. He knelt beside Butcher, and within minutes they had unearthed a second large green-encrusted plate. This one was a shade smaller than the first, and deeper. More of a bowl than a dish.

Ford stood up and held the new find in his hands. Another heavy one. And now he knew for certain they were onto something absolutely tremendous. They were onto Roman treasure, and almost without question it was pure silver. Two things pointed to it being pure silver. First the weight, and second, the particular type of green crust caused by oxidation.

How often is a piece of Roman silver discovered in the world?

Almost never anymore.

And have pieces as large as this *ever* been unearthed before?

Ford wasn't sure, but he very much doubted it.

Worth millions it must be.

Worth literally millions of pounds.

His breath, coming fast, was making little white clouds in the freezing atmosphere.

"There's still more down here, Mr. Ford," Butcher was saying. "I can feel bits of it all over the place. You'll need the spade again."

The third piece they got out was another large plate, somewhat similar to the first. Ford placed it in the barley stubble with the other two.

Then Butcher felt the first flake of snow upon his cheek, and he looked up and saw over to the northeast a great white curtain drawn across the sky, a solid wall of snow flying forward on the wings of the wind.

"Here she comes!" he said, and Ford looked around and saw the snow moving down upon them and said, "It's a blizzard. It's a filthy, stinking blizzard!"

The two men stared at the blizzard as it raced across the fens toward them. Then it was on them, and all around was snow and snowflakes, white wind with snowflakes slanting in the wind and snowflakes in the eyes and ears and mouth and down the neck and all around. And when Butcher glanced down at the ground a few seconds later it was already white.

"That's all we want," Ford said. "A filthy, rotten, stinking blizzard," and he shivered and sunk his sharp and foxy face deeper into the collar of his coat. "Come on," he said. "See if there's any more."

Butcher knelt down again and poked around in the soil, then in the slow and casual manner of a man having a lucky dip in a barrel of sawdust, he pulled out another plate and held it out to Ford, who took it and put it down beside the rest. Now Ford knelt down beside Butcher and began to dip into the soil with him.

For a whole hour the two men stayed out there digging and scratching in that three-foot patch of soil. And during that hour they found and laid upon the ground beside them *no less than thirty-three separate pieces!* There were dishes, bowls, goblets, spoons, ladles and several other things, all of them crusted over but each one recognizable for what it was. And all the while the blizzard swirled around them and the snow gathered in little mounds on their caps and on their shoulders and the flakes melted on their faces so that rivers of icy water trickled down their necks. A large globule of half-frozen liquid dangled continually, like a snowdrop, from the end of Ford's pointed nose.

They worked in silence. It was too cold to speak. And as one precious article after the other was unearthed, Ford laid them carefully on the ground in rows, pausing every now and then to wipe the snow away from a dish or a spoon that was in danger of being completely covered.

At last Ford said, "That's the lot, I think."

"Yes."

Ford stood up and stamped his feet on the ground. "Got a sack in the tractor?" he said, and while Butcher walked over to fetch the sack, he turned and gazed upon the three-and-thirty pieces lying in the snow at his feet. He counted them again. If they were silver, which they surely must be, and if they were Roman, which they undoubtedly were, then this was a discovery that would rock the world.

Butcher called to him from the tractor, "It's only a dirty old sack."

"It'll do."

Butcher brought the sack over and held it open while Ford carefully put the articles into it. They all went in except one. The massive two-foot plate was too large for the neck of the sack.

The two men were really cold now. For over an hour they had knelt and scratched about out there in the open field with the blizzard swirling around them. Already, nearly six inches of snow had fallen. Butcher was half frozen. His cheeks were dead white, blotched with blue; his feet were numb like wood, and when he moved his legs he could not feel the ground beneath him. He was much colder than Ford. Butcher's coat and clothes were not so thick, and ever since early morning he had been sitting high up on the seat of the tractor, exposed to the bitter wind. His blue-white face was tight and unmoving. All he wanted was to get home to his family and to the fire that he knew would be burning in the grate.

Ford, on the other hand, was not thinking about the cold. His mind was concentrated solely upon one thing—how to get possession of this fabulous treasure. His position, as he knew very well, was not a strong one.

In England there is a very curious law about finding any kind of gold or silver treasure. This law goes back hundreds of years and is still strictly enforced today. The law states that if a person digs up out of the ground, even out of his own garden, a piece of metal that is either *gold* or *silver*, it automatically becomes what is known as treasure trove and is the property of the Crown. The Crown doesn't in these days mean the actual king or queen. It means the country or the government. The law also states that it is a criminal offense to conceal such a find. You are simply not allowed to hide the stuff and keep it for yourself. You must report it at once, preferably to the police. And if you do report it at once, you as the finder will be entitled to receive from the government in money the full amount of the market value of the article. You are not required to report the digging up of other metals. You are allowed to find as much valuable pewter, bronze, copper or even platinum as you wish, and you can keep it all; but not gold or silver.

The other curious part of this curious law is this: it is the person who *discovers* the treasure in the first place who gets the reward from the government. The owner of the land gets nothing—unless of course the finder is trespassing on the land when he makes the discovery. But if the finder of the treasure has been hired by the owner to do a job on his land, then he, the finder, gets all the reward.

In this case, the finder was Gordon Butcher. Furthermore, he was not trespassing. He was performing a job that he had been hired to do. This treasure therefore belonged to Butcher and to no one else. All he had to do was take it and show it to an expert who would immediately identify it as silver, then turn it in to the police. In time, he would receive from the government 100 percent of its value—perhaps a million pounds sterling.

All this left Ford out in the cold, and Ford knew it. He had no rights whatsoever to the treasure by law. Thus, as he must have told himself at the time, his only chance of getting hold of the stuff for himself lay in the fact that Butcher was an ignorant man who didn't know the law and who did not anyway have the faintest idea of the value of the find. The probability was that in a few days Butcher would forget all about it. He was too simpleminded a fellow, too artless, too trusting, too unselfish to give the matter much thought.

Now, out there in the desolate snow-swept field, Ford bent down and took hold of the huge dish with one hand. He raised it but he did not lift it. The lower rim remained resting in the snow. With his other hand, he grasped the top of the sack. He didn't lift that either. He just held it. And there he stooped amid the swirling snowflakes, both hands embracing, as it were, the treasure, but not actually taking it. It was a subtle and a canny gesture. It managed somehow to signify ownership before ownership had been discussed. A child plays the same game when he reaches out and closes his fingers over the biggest chocolate éclair

on the plate and then says, "Can I have this one, Mummy?"
He's already got it.

"Well, Gordon," Ford said, stooping over, holding the
sack and the great dish in his gloved fingers. "I don't suppose you want any of this old stuff."

It was not a question. It was a statement of fact framed
as a question.

The blizzard was still raging. The snow was falling so
densely, the two men could hardly see one another.

"You ought to get along home and warm yourself up,"
Ford went on. "You look frozen to death."

"I *feel* frozen to death," Butcher said.

"Then you get on that tractor quick and hurry home,"
said the thoughtful, kindhearted Ford. "Leave the plow here
and leave your bike at my place. The important thing is to
get back and warm yourself up before you catch pneumonia."

"I think that's just what I will do, Mr. Ford," Butcher
said. "Can you manage all right with that sack? It's mighty
heavy."

"I might not even bother about it today," Ford said casually. "I just might leave it here and come back for it another time. Rusty old stuff."

"So long then, Mr. Ford."

" 'Bye, Gordon."

Gordon Butcher mounted the tractor and drove away into
the blizzard.

Ford hoisted the sack onto his shoulder, and then, not
without difficulty he lifted the massive dish with his other
hand and tucked it under his arm.

I am carrying, he told himself, as he trudged through
the snow, I am now carrying what is probably the biggest
treasure ever dug up in the whole history of England.

When Gordon Butcher came stamping and blowing
through the back door of his small brick house late that

afternoon, his wife was ironing by the fire. She looked up and saw his blue-white face and snow-encrusted clothes.

"My goodness, Gordon, you look froze to death!" she cried.

"I am," he said. "Help me off with these clothes, love. My fingers aren't hardly working at all."

She took off his gloves, his coat, his jacket, his wet shirt. She pulled off his boots and socks. She fetched a towel and rubbed his chest and shoulders vigorously all over to restore the circulation. She rubbed his feet.

"Sit down there by the fire," she said, "and I'll get you a hot cup of tea."

Later, when he was settled comfortably in the warmth with dry clothes on his back and the mug of tea in his hand, he told her what had happened that afternoon.

"He's a foxy one, that Mr. Ford," she said, not looking up from her ironing. "I never did like him."

"He got pretty excited about it all, I can tell you that," Gordon Butcher said. "Jumpy as a jackrabbit he was."

"That may be," she said. "But you ought to have had more sense than to go crawling about on your hands and knees in a freezing blizzard just because Mr. Ford said to do it."

"I'm all right," Gordon Butcher said. "I'm warming up nicely now."

And that, believe it or not, was about the last time the subject of the treasure was discussed in the Butcher household for some years.

The reader should be reminded here that this was wartime, 1942. Britain was totally absorbed in the desperate war against Hitler and Mussolini. Germany was bombing England, and England was bombing Germany, and nearly every night Gordon Butcher heard the roar of engines from the big airbase at nearby Mildenhall as the bombers took off for Hamburg, Berlin, Kiel, Wilhelmshaven or Frankfurt.

Sometimes he would wake in the early hours and hear them coming home, and sometimes the Germans flew over to bomb the base, and the Butcher house would shake with the crumph and crash of bombs not far away.

Butcher himself was exempt from military service. He was a farmer, a skilled plowman, and they had told him when he volunteered for the army in 1939 that he was not wanted. The island's food supplies must be kept going, they said, and it was vital that men like him stay on their jobs and cultivate the land.

Ford, being in the same business, was also exempt. He was a bachelor, living alone, and he was thus able to live a secret life and do secret things within the walls of his home.

And so, on that terrible snowy afternoon when they dug up the treasure, Ford carried it home and laid everything out on a table in the back room.

Thirty-three separate pieces! They covered the entire table. And by the look of it, they were in marvelous condition. Silver does not rust. The green crust of oxidation can even be a protection for the surface of the metal underneath. And with care, it could all be removed.

Ford decided to use an ordinary domestic silver polish known as Silvo, and he bought a large stock of it from the ironmonger's shop in Mildenhall. He took first the great two-foot plate, which weighed more than eighteen pounds. He worked on it in the evenings. He soaked it all over with Silvo. He rubbed and rubbed. He worked patiently on this single dish every night for more than sixteen weeks.

At last, one memorable evening, there showed beneath his rubbing a small area of shining silver, and on the silver, raised up and beautifully worked, there was a part of a man's head.

He kept at it, and gradually the little patch of shining metal spread and spread, the blue-green crust crept outward to the edges of the plate until finally the top surface of the great dish lay before him in its full glory, covered all over with a wondrous pattern of animals and men and many odd legendary things.

Ford was astounded by the beauty of the great plate. It was filled with life and movement. There was a fierce face with tangled hair, a dancing goat with a human head, there were men and women and animals of many kinds cavorting around the rim, and no doubt all of them told a story.

Next he set about cleaning the reverse side of the plate. Weeks and weeks it took. And when the work was completed and the whole plate on both sides was shining like a star, he placed it safely in the lower cupboard of his big oak sideboard and locked the cupboard door.

One by one, he tackled the remaining thirty-two pieces. A mania had taken hold of him now, a fierce compulsion to make every item shine in all its silver brilliance. He wanted to see all thirty-three pieces laid out on the big table in a dazzling array of silver. He wanted that more than anything else, and he worked desperately hard to achieve his wish.

He cleaned the two smaller dishes next, then the large fluted bowl, then the five long-handled ladles, the goblets, the wine cups, the spoons. Every single piece was cleaned with equal care and made to shine with equal brilliance; and when they were all done two years had passed, and it was 1944.

But no strangers were allowed to look. Ford discussed the matter with no man or woman, and Rolfe, the owner of the plot on Thistley Green where the treasure had been found, knew nothing except that Ford, or someone Ford had hired, had plowed his land extremely well and very deep.

One can guess why Ford hid the treasure instead of reporting it to the police as treasure trove. Had he reported it, it would have been taken away and Gordon Butcher would have been rewarded as the finder. Rewarded with a fortune. So the only thing Ford could do was to hang on to it and hide it in the hope, presumably, of selling it quietly to some dealer or collector at a later date.

It is possible, of course, to take a more charitable view and assume that Ford kept the treasure solely because he loved beautiful things and wanted to have them around him. No one will ever know the true answer.

Another year went by.

The war against Hitler was won.

And then, in 1946, just after Easter, there was a knock on the door of Ford's house. Ford opened it.

"Why hello, Mr. Ford. How are you after all these years?"

"Hello, Dr. Fawcett," Ford said. "You been keeping all right?"

"I'm fine, thank you," Dr. Fawcett said. "It's been a long time, hasn't it?"

"Yes," Ford said. "That old war kept us all pretty busy."

"May I come in?" Dr. Fawcett asked.

"Of course," Ford said. "Come on in."

Dr. Hugh Alderson Fawcett was a keen and learned archaeologist who before the war had made a point of visiting Ford once a year in search of old stones or arrowheads. Ford had usually collected a batch of such items during the twelve months and he was always willing to sell them to Fawcett. They were seldom of great value, but now and again something quite good had turned up.

"Well," said Fawcett, taking off his coat in the little hall, "Well, well, well. It's been nearly seven years since I was here last."

"Yes, it's been a long time," Ford said.

Ford led him into the front room and showed him a box of flint arrowheads that had been picked up in the district. Some were good, others not so good. Fawcett picked through them, sorted them, and a deal was made.

"Nothing else?"

"No, I don't think so."

Ford wished fervently that Dr. Fawcett had never come. He wished even more fervently that he would go away.

It was at this point that Ford noticed something that made him sweat. He saw suddenly that he had left lying on the mantle over the fireplace the two most beautiful of the Roman spoons from the treasure hoard. These spoons had fascinated him because each was inscribed with the name of a Roman girl child. One was Pascentia, the other was Pappitedo. Rather lovely names.

Ford, sweating with fear, tried to place himself between Dr. Fawcett and the mantlepiece. He might even, he thought, be able to slip the spoons into his pocket if he got the chance.

He didn't get the chance.

Perhaps Ford had polished them so well that a little flash of reflected light from the silver caught the doctor's eye. Who knows? The fact remains that Fawcett saw them. The moment he saw them, he pounced like a tiger.

"Great heavens alive!" he cried. "What are these?"

"Pewter," Ford said, sweating more than ever. "Just a couple of old pewter spoons."

"Pewter?" cried Fawcett, turning one of the spoons over in his fingers. "Pewter! You call this *pewter?*"

"That's right," Ford said. "It's pewter."

"You know what this is?" Fawcett said, his voice going high with excitement. "Shall I tell you what this *really* is?"

"You don't have to tell me," Ford said, truculent. "I know what it is. It's old pewter. And quite nice, too."

Fawcett was reading the inscription in Roman letters on the scoop of the spoon. "Pappitedo!" he cried.

"What's that mean?" Ford asked him.

Fawcett picked up the other spoon. "Pascentia," he said.

"Beautiful! These are the names of Roman children! And these spoons, my friend, are made of solid silver! Solid Roman silver!"

"Not possible," Ford said.

"They're magnificent!" Fawcett cried out, going into raptures. "They're perfect! They're unbelievable! Where on earth did you find them? It's most important to know where you found them! Was there anything else?" Fawcett was hopping about all over the room.

"Well . . ." Ford said, licking dry lips.

"You must report them at once!" Fawcett cried. "They're treasure trove! The British Museum is going to want these and that's for certain! How long have you had them?"

"Just a little while," Ford told him.

"And *who* found them?" Fawcett asked, looking straight at him. "Did you find them yourself or did you get them from somebody else? This is vital! The finder will be able to tell us all about it!"

Ford felt the walls of the room closing in on him and he didn't quite know what to do.

"Come on, man! Surely you know where you got them! Every detail will have to come out when you hand them in. Promise me you'll go to the police with them at once!"

"Well . . ." Ford said.

"If you don't, then I'm afraid I shall be forced to report it myself," Fawcett told him. "It's my duty."

The game was up now, and Ford knew it. A thousand questions would be asked. How did you find it? When did you find it? What were you doing? Where was the exact spot? Whose land were you plowing? And sooner or later, inevitably, the name of Gordon Butcher would have to come into it. It was unavoidable. And then, when Butcher was questioned, he would remember the size of the hoard and tell them all about it.

So the game was up. And the only thing to do at this point was to unlock the doors of the big sideboard and show the entire hoard to Dr. Fawcett.

Ford's excuse for keeping it all and not turning it in would have to be that he thought it was pewter. So long as he stuck to that, he told himself, they couldn't do anything to him.

Dr. Fawcett would probably have a heart attack when he saw what there was in that cupboard.

"There is actually quite a bit more of it," Ford said.

"Where?" cried Fawcett, spinning round. "Where, man, where? Lead me to it!"

"I really thought it was pewter," Ford said, moving slowly and very reluctantly forward to the oak sideboard. "Otherwise, I would naturally have reported it at once."

He bent down and unlocked the lower doors of the sideboard. He opened the doors.

And then Dr. Hugh Alderson Fawcett very nearly did have a heart attack. He flung himself on his knees. He gasped. He choked. He began spluttering like an old kettle. He reached out for the great silver dish. He took it. He held it in shaking hands and his face went as white as snow. He didn't speak. He couldn't. He was literally—physically and mentally—struck absolutely dumb by the sight of the treasure.

The interesting part of the story ends here. The rest is routine. Ford went to Mildenhall police station and made a report. The police came at once and collected all thirty-three pieces, and they were sent under guard to the British Museum for examination.

Then an urgent message from the museum to the Mildenhall police. It was far and away the finest Roman silver ever found in the British Isles. It was of enormous value. The museum (which is really a public governmental institution) wished to acquire it. In fact, they insisted upon acquiring it.

The wheels of the law began to turn. An official inquest and hearing was arranged at the nearest large town, Bury St. Edmunds. The silver was moved there under special police guard. Ford was summoned to appear before the coroner and a jury of fourteen, while Gordon Butcher, that good and quiet man, was ordered also to present himself to give evidence.

On Monday, July 1, 1946, the hearing took place, and the coroner cross-questioned Ford closely.

"You thought it was pewter?"

"Yes."

"Even after you had cleaned it?"

"Yes."

"You took no steps to inform any experts of the find?"

"No."

"What did you intend to do with the articles?"

"Nothing. Just keep them."

And when he had concluded his evidence, Ford asked permission to go outside into the fresh air because he said he felt faint. Nobody was surprised.

Then Butcher was called, and in a few simple words he told of his part in the affair.

Dr. Fawcett gave his evidence, as did several other learned archaeologists, all of whom testified to the extreme rarity of the treasure. They said that it was of the fourth century after Christ; that it was the table silver of a wealthy Roman family; that it had probably been buried by the owner's bailiff to save it from the Picts and Scots, who swept down from the north in about A.D. 365 and laid waste many Roman settlements. The man who buried it had probably been liquidated either by a Pict or a Scot, and the treasure had remained concealed a foot below the soil ever since. The workmanship, said the experts, was magnificent.

Some of it may have been executed in England, but more probably the articles were made in Italy or in Egypt. The great plate was of course the finest piece. The head in the center was that of Neptune, the sea god, with dolphins in his hair and seaweed in his beard. All around him, sea nymphs and sea monsters gamboled. On the broad rim of the plate stood Bacchus and his attendants. There was wine and revelry. Hercules was there, quite drunk, supported by two satyrs, his lion's skin fallen from his shoulders. Pan was there too, dancing upon his goat-legs with his pipes in his hand. And everywhere there were Maenads, female devotees of Bacchus, rather tipsy women.

The court was told also that several of the spoons bore the monogram of Christ (*Chi-Rho*) and that the two that were inscribed with the names Pascentia and Pappitedo were undoubtedly christening presents.

The experts concluded their evidence, and the court adjourned. Soon the jury returned, and their verdict was astonishing. No blame was attached to anyone for anything, although the finder of the treasure was no longer entitled to receive full compensation from the Crown because the find had not been declared at once. Nevertheless, there would probably be a measure of compensation paid, and with this in view, the finders were declared to be jointly Ford and Butcher.

Not Butcher. Ford and Butcher.

There is no more to tell other than that the treasure was acquired by the British Museum, where it now stands proudly displayed in a large glass case for all to see. And already people have traveled great distances to go and look upon those lovely things that Gordon Butcher found beneath his plow on that cold and windy winter afternoon. One day, a book or two will be compiled about them, full of suppositions and abstruse conclusions, and men who move

in archaeological circles will talk forever about the Treasure
of Mildenhall.

As a gesture, the museum rewarded the co-finders with
one thousand pounds each. Butcher, the true finder, was
happy and surprised to receive so much money. He did not
realize that, had he been allowed to take the treasure home
originally, he would almost certainly have revealed its ex-
istence and would thus have become eligible to receive 100
percent of its value, which could have been anything between half a million and a million pounds.

Nobody knows what Ford thought about it all. He must
have been relieved and perhaps somewhat surprised when
he heard that the court had believed his story about pewter.
But above all, he must have been shattered by the loss of
his great treasure. For the rest of his life he would be kicking himself for leaving those two spoons on the mantle
above the fireplace for Dr. Fawcett to see.

The Swan

Ernie had been given a .22-caliber rifle for his birthday.

His father, who was already slouching on the sofa watching television at nine thirty on this Saturday morning, said, "Let's see what you can pot, boy. Make yourself useful. Bring us back a rabbit for supper."

"There's rabbits in that big field the other side of the lake," Ernie said. "I seen 'em."

"Then go out and nab one," the father said, picking breakfast from between his front teeth with a split matchstick. "Go out and nab us a rabbit."

"I'll get yer two," Ernie said.

"And on the way back," the father said, "get me a quart bottle of brown ale."

"Gimme the money, then," Ernie said.

The father, without taking his eyes from the TV screen, fished in his pocket for a pound note. "And don't try pinchin' the change like you did last time," he said. "You'll get a thick ear if you do, birthday or no birthday."

"Don't worry," Ernie said.

"And if you want to practice and get your eye in with that gun," the father said, "birds is best. See 'ow many spadgers you can knock down, right?"

"Right," Ernie said. "There's spadgers all the way up the lane in the 'edges. Spadgers is easy."

"If you think spadgers is easy," the father said, "go get yourself a jenny wren. Jenny wrens is 'alf the size of spadgers and they never sit still for one second. Get yourself a jenny wren before you start shootin' yer mouth off about 'ow clever you is."

"Now Albert," his wife said, looking up from the sink. "That's not nice, shootin' little birds in the nestin' season. I don't mind rabbits, but little birds in the nestin' season is another thing altogether."

"Shut your mouth," the father said. "Nobody's askin' your opinion. And listen to me, boy," he said to Ernie. "Don't go wavin' that thing about in the street because you ain't got no license. Stick it down your trouser leg till you're out in the country, right?"

"Don't worry," Ernie said. He took the gun and the box of bullets and went out to see what he could kill. He was a big lout of a boy, fifteen years old this birthday. Like his truck-driver father, he had small slitty eyes set very close together near the top of the nose. His mouth was loose, the lips often wet. Brought up in a household where physical violence was an everyday occurrence, he was himself an extremely violent person. Most Saturday afternoons, he and a gang of friends traveled by train or bus to soccer matches, and if they didn't manage to get into a bloody fight before they returned home, they considered it a wasted day. He took great pleasure in catching small boys after school and twisting their arms behind their backs. Then he would order them to say insulting and filthy things about their own parents.

"Ow! Please don't, Ernie! Please!"

"Say it or I'll twist your arm off!"

They always said it. Then he would give the arm an extra twist, and the victim would go off in tears.

Ernie's best friend was called Raymond. He lived four doors away, and he, too, was a big boy for his age. But while Ernie was heavy and loutish, Raymond was tall, slim and muscular.

Outside Raymond's house, Ernie put two fingers in his mouth and gave a long, shrill whistle. Raymond came out.

"Look what I got for me birthday," Ernie said, showing the gun.

"Cripes!" Raymond said. "We can have some fun with that!"

"Come on, then," Ernie said. "We're goin' up to the big field the other side of the lake and get us a rabbit."

The two boys set off. This was a Saturday morning in May, and the countryside was beautiful around the small village where the boys lived. The chestnut trees were in full flower and the hawthorn was white along the hedges. To reach the big rabbit field, Ernie and Raymond had first to walk down a narrow hedgy lane for half a mile. Then they must cross the railway line, and go around the big lake where wild ducks and moorhens and coots and ring-ouzels lived. Beyond the lake, over the hill and down the other side, lay the rabbit field. This was all private land belonging to Douglas Highton, and the lake itself was a sanctuary for waterfowl.

All the way up the lane, they took turns with the gun, potting at small birds in the hedges. Ernie got a bullfinch and a hedge sparrow. Raymond got a second bullfinch, a whitethroat and a yellowhammer. As each bird was killed, they tied it by the legs to a line of string. Raymond never went anywhere without a big ball of string in his jacket pocket, and a knife. Now they had five little birds dangling on the line of string.

"You know something," Raymond said. "We can eat these."

"Don't talk so daft," Ernie said. "There's not enough meat on one of those to feed a woodlouse."

"There is, too," Raymond said. "The Frenchies eat 'em and so do the Eyeties. Mr. Sanders told us about it in class. He said the Frenchies and the Eyeties put up nets and catch 'em by the million and then they eat 'em."

"All right, then," Ernie said. "Let's see 'ow many we can get. Then we'll take 'em 'ome and put 'em in the rabbit stew."

As they progressed up the lane, they shot at every little bird they saw. By the time they got to the railway line, they had fourteen small dead birds dangling on the line of string.

"Hey!" whispered Ernie, pointing with a long arm. "Look over there!"

There was a group of trees and bushes alongside the railway line, and beside one of the bushes stood a small boy. He was looking up into the branches of an old tree through a pair of binoculars.

"You know who that is?" Raymond whispered back. "It's that little twerp Watson."

"You're right!" Ernie whispered. "It's Watson, the scum of the earth!"

Peter Watson was always the enemy. Ernie and Raymond detested him because he was nearly everything that they were not. He had a small, frail body. His face was freckled, and he wore spectacles with thick lenses. He was a brilliant pupil, already in the senior class at school although he was only thirteen. He loved music and played the piano well. He was no good at games. He was quiet and polite. His clothes, although patched and darned, were always clean. And his father did not drive a truck or work in a factory. He worked in the bank.

"Let's give the little perisher a fright," Ernie whispered.

The two bigger boys crept up close to the small boy, who didn't see them because he still had the binoculars to his eyes.

"'*Ands up!*" shouted Ernie, pointing the gun.

Peter Watson jumped. He lowered the binoculars and stared through his spectacles at the two intruders.

"Go on!" Ernie shouted. "Stick 'em up!"

"I wouldn't point that gun if I were you," Peter Watson said.

"*We're* givin' the orders round 'ere!" Ernie said.

"So stick 'em up," Raymond said, "unless you want a slug in the guts!"

Peter Watson stood quite still, holding the binoculars in front of him with both hands. He looked at Raymond. Then he looked at Ernie. He was not afraid, but he knew better than to play the fool with these two. He had suffered a good deal from their attentions over the years.

"What do you want?" he asked.

"*I want you to stick 'em up!*" Ernie yelled at him. "Can't you understand English?"

Peter Watson didn't move.

"I'll count to five," Ernie said, "and if they're not up by then, you get it in the guts. One . . . two . . . three . . ."

Peter Watson raised his arms slowly above his head. It was the only sensible thing to do. Raymond stepped forward and snatched the binoculars from his hand. "What's this?" he snapped. "Who you spyin' on?"

"Nobody."

"Don't lie, Watson. Them things is used for spyin'! I'll bet you was spyin' on us! That's right, ain't it? Confess it!"

"I certainly wasn't spying on you."

"Give 'im a clip over the ear," Ernie said. "Teach 'im not to lie to us."

"I'll do that in a minute," Raymond said. "I'm just workin' meself up."

Peter Watson considered the possibility of trying to escape. All he could do would be to turn and run, and that was pointless. They'd catch him in seconds. And if he shouted for help, there was no one to hear him. All he could do, therefore, was to keep calm and try to talk his way out.

"Keep them 'ands up!" Ernie barked, waving the barrel of the gun gently from side to side the way he had seen it done by gangsters on television. "Go on, laddie, reach!"

Peter did as he was told.

"So 'oo was you spyin' on?" Raymond asked. "Out with it!"

"I was watching a green woodpecker," Peter said.

"A what?"

"A male green woodpecker. He was tapping the trunk of that old dead tree, searching for grubs."

"Where is 'ee?" Ernie snapped, raising his gun. "I'll 'ave 'im!"

"No, you won't," Peter said, looking at the string of tiny birds slung over Raymond's shoulder. "He flew off the moment you shouted. Woodpeckers are extremely timid."

"What you watchin' 'im for?" Raymond asked suspiciously. "What's the point? Don't you 'ave nothin' better to do?"

"It's fun watching birds," Peter said. "It's a lot more fun than shooting them."

"Why you cheeky little bleeder!" Ernie cried. "So you don't like us shootin' birds, eh? Is that what you're sayin'?"

"I think it's absolutely pointless."

"You don't like anything we do, isn't that right?" Raymond said.

Peter didn't answer.

"Well, let me tell *you* something," Raymond went on. "We don't like anything you do either."

Peter's arms were beginning to ache. He decided to take a risk. Slowly, he lowered them to his sides.

"Up!" yelled Ernie. "Get 'em up!"

"What if I refuse?"

"Blimey! You got a ruddy nerve, ain't you?" Ernie said. "I'm tellin' you for the last time, if you don't stick 'em up I'll pull the trigger!"

"That would be a criminal act," Peter said. "It would be a case for the police."

"And you'd be a case for the 'ospital!" Ernie said.

"Go ahead and shoot," Peter said. "Then they'll send you to Borstal. That's prison."

He saw Ernie hesitate.

"You're really askin' for it, ain't you?" Raymond said.

"I'm simply asking to be let alone," Peter said. "I haven't done you any harm."

"You're a stuck-up little squirt," Ernie said. "That's exactly what you are, a stuck-up little squirt."

Raymond leaned over and whispered something in Ernie's ear. Ernie listened intently. Then he slapped his thigh and said, "I like it! It's a great idea!"

Ernie placed his gun on the ground and advanced upon the small boy. He grabbed him and threw him to the ground. Raymond took the roll of string from his pocket and cut off a length of it. Together, they forced the boy's arms in front of him and tied his wrists together tight.

"Now the legs," Raymond said. Peter struggled and received a punch in the stomach. This winded him, and he lay still. Next, they tied his ankles together with more string. He was now trussed up like a chicken and completely helpless.

Ernie picked up his gun, and then, with his other hand, he grabbed one of Peter's arms. Raymond grabbed the other arm and together they began to drag the boy over the grass toward the railway line.

Peter kept absolutely quiet. Whatever it was they were up to, talking to them wasn't going to help matters.

They dragged their victim down the embankment and onto the railway tracks themselves. Then one took the arms and the other the feet and they lifted him up and laid him down again lengthwise right between two rails.

"You're mad!" Peter said. "You can't do this!"

"'Oo says we can't? This is just a little lesson we're teachin' you not to be cheeky."

"More string," Ernie said.

Raymond produced the ball of string, and the two larger boys now proceeded to tie their victim down in such a way that he couldn't wriggle away from between the rails. They did this by looping string around each of his arms and then threading the string under the rails on either side. They did the same with his middle body and his ankles. When they had finished, Peter Watson was strung down helpless and virtually immobile between the rails. The only parts of his body he could move to any extent were his head and feet.

Ernie and Raymond stepped back to survey their handiwork. "We done a nice job," Ernie said.

"There's trains every 'arf 'our on this line," Raymond said. "We ain't gonna 'ave long to wait."

"This is murder!" cried the small boy lying between the rails.

"No it ain't," Raymond told him. "It ain't anything of the sort."

"Let me go! Please let me go! I'll be killed if a train comes along!"

"If you *are* killed, sonny boy," Ernie said, "it'll be your own ruddy fault and I'll tell you why. Because if you lift your 'ead up like you're doin' now, then you've 'ad it, chum! You keep down flat and you might just possibly get away with it. On the other 'and, you might not because I ain't exactly sure 'ow much clearance them trains've got underneath. You 'appen to know, Raymond, 'ow much clearance them trains got underneath?"

"Very little," Raymond said. "They're built ever so close to the ground."

"Might be enough and it might not," Ernie said.

"Let's put it this way," Raymond said. "It'd probably

just about be enough for an *ordinary* person like me or you, Ernie. But Mister Watson 'ere I'm not so sure about and I'll tell you why."

"Tell me," Ernie said, egging him on.

"Mister Watson 'ere's got an extra big head, that's why. 'Ee's so flippin' big-'eaded I personally think the bottom bit of the train's goin' to scrape 'im whatever 'appens. I'm not sayin' it's goin' to take 'is 'ead off, mind you. In fact, I'm pretty sure it ain't goin' to do that. But it's goin' to give 'is face a good old scrapin' over. You can be quite sure of that."

"I think you're right," Ernie said.

"It don't do," Raymond said, "to 'ave a great big swollen 'ead full of brains if you're lyin' on the railway tracks with a train comin' toward you. That's right, ain't it, Ernie?"

"That's right," Ernie said.

The two bigger boys climbed back up the embankment and sat on the grass behind some bushes. Ernie produced a pack of cigarettes, and they both lit up.

Peter Watson, lying helpless between the rails, realized now that they were not going to release him. These were dangerous, crazy boys. They lived for the moment and never considered the consequences. I must try to keep calm and think, Peter told himself. He lay there, quite still, weighing his chances. His chances were good. The highest part of him was his head and the highest part of his head was his nose. He estimated the end of his nose was sticking up about four inches above the rails. Was that too much? He wasn't quite sure what clearance these modern diesels had above the ground. It certainly wasn't very much. The back of his head was resting upon loose gravel in between two sleepers. He must try to burrow down a little into the gravel. So he began to wriggle his head from side to side, pushing the gravel away and gradually making for himself a small indentation, a hole in the gravel. In the end, he reckoned he had lowered his head an extra two inches. That would do for the head. But what about the feet. They were sticking up, too. He took care of that by swinging the two tied-together feet over to one side so that they lay almost flat.

He waited for the train to come.

Would the driver see him? It was very unlikely, for this was the main line, London, Doncaster, York, Newcastle and Scotland, and they used huge long engines in which the driver sat in a cab way back and kept an eye open only for the signals. Along this stretch of the track they traveled around eightly miles an hour. Peter knew that. He had sat on the bank many times watching them. When he was younger, he used to keep a record of their numbers in a little book, and sometimes the engines had names written on their sides in gold letters.

Either way, he told himself, it was going to be a terrifying business. The noise would be deafening, and the swish of the eighty-mile-an-hour wind wouldn't be much fun either. He wondered for a moment whether there would be any kind of vacuum created underneath the train as it rushed over him, sucking him upward. There might well be. So whatever happened, he must concentrate everything upon pressing his entire body against the ground. Don't go limp. Keep stiff and tense and press down into the ground.

"How're you doin', ratface?" one of them called out to him from the bushes above. "What's it like, waitin' for the execution?"

He decided not to answer. He watched the blue sky above his head where a single huge cumulus cloud was drifting slowly from left to right. And to keep his mind off the thing that was going to happen soon, he played a game that his father had taught him long ago on a hot summer's day when they were lying on their backs in the grass above the cliffs at Beachy Head. The game was to look for strange faces in the folds and shadows and billows of a cumulus cloud. If you looked hard enough, his father had said, you would always find a face of some sort up there. Peter let his eyes travel slowly over the cloud. In one place, he found a one-eyed man with a beard. In another, there was a long-chinned laughing witch. An airplane came across the cloud traveling from east to west. It was a small high-winged monoplane with a red fuselage. An old Piper Cub, he thought it was. He watched it until it disappeared.

And then, quite suddenly, he heard a curious little vibrating sound coming from the rails on either side of him. It was very soft, this sound, scarcely audible, a tiny little humming, thrumming whisper that seemed to be coming along the rails from far away.

That's a train, he told himself.

The vibrating along the rails grew louder, then louder still. He raised his head and looked down the long and absolutely straight railway track that stretched away for a mile or more into the distance. It was then that he saw the train. At first it was only a speck, a faraway black dot, but in those few seconds that he kept his head raised, the dot grew bigger and bigger, and it began to take shape, and soon it was no longer a dot but the big, square, blunt front-end of a diesel express. Peter dropped his head and pressed it down hard into the small hole he had dug for it in the gravel. He swung his feet over to one side. He shut his eyes tight and tried to sink his body into the ground.

The train came over him like an explosion. It was as though a gun had gone off in his head. And with the explosion came a tearing, screaming wind that was like a hurricane blowing down his nostrils and into his lungs. The noise was shattering. The wind choked him. He felt as if he were being eaten alive and swallowed up in the belly of a screaming murderous monster.

And then it was over. The train had gone. Peter opened his eyes and saw the blue sky and the big white cloud still drifting overhead. It was all over now and he had done it. He had survived.

"It missed 'im," said a voice.

"What a pity," said another voice.

He glanced sideways and saw the two large louts standing over him.

"Cut 'im loose," Ernie said.

Raymond cut the strings binding him to the rails on either side.

"Undo 'is feet so 'ee can walk, but keep 'is 'ands tied," Ernie said.

Raymond cut the string around his ankles.

"Get up," Ernie said.

Peter got to his feet.

"You're still a prisoner, matey," Ernie said.

"What about them rabbits?" Raymond asked. "I thought we was goin' to try for a few rabbits?"

"Plenty of time for that," Ernie answered. "I just thought we'd push the little bleeder into the lake on the way."

"Good," Raymond said. "Cool 'im down."

"You've had your fun," Peter Watson said. "Why don't you let me go now?"

"Because you're a prisoner," Ernie said. "And you ain't just no ordinary prisoner neither. You're a spy. And you know what 'appens to spies when they get caught, don't you? They get put up against the wall and shot."

Peter didn't say any more after that. There was no point at all in provoking these two. The less he said to them and the less he resisted them, the more chance he would have of escaping injury. He had no doubt whatsoever that in their present mood they were capable of doing him quite serious bodily harm. He knew for a fact that Ernie had once broken little Wally Simpson's arm after school, and Wally's parents had gone to the police. He had also heard Raymond boasting about what he called "putting the boot in" at the soccer matches they went to. This, he understood, meant kicking someone in the face or body when he was lying on the ground. They were hooligans, these two, and from what Peter read in his father's newspaper nearly every day, they were not by any means on their own. It seemed the whole country was full of hooligans. They wrecked the interiors of trains, they fought pitched battles in the streets with knives and bicycle chains and metal clubs, they attacked pedestrians, especially other young boys walking alone, and they smashed up roadside cafés. Ernie and Raymond, though perhaps not quite yet fully qualified hooligans, were most definitely on their way.

Therefore, Peter told himself, he must continue to be passive. Don't insult them. Do not aggravate them in any way. And above all, do not try to take them on physically. Then, hopefully, in the end, they might become bored with this nasty little game and go off to shoot rabbits.

The two larger boys had each taken hold of one of Peter's arms and they were marching him across the next field toward the lake. The prisoner's wrists were still tied together in front of him. Ernie carried the gun in his spare hand. Raymond carried the binoculars he had taken from Peter. They came to the lake.

The lake was beautiful on this golden May morning. It was a long and fairly narrow lake with tall willow trees growing here and there along its banks. In the middle, the water was clear and clean, but nearer to the land there was a forest of reeds and bullrushes.

Ernie and Raymond marched their prisoner to the edge of the lake, and there they stopped.

"Now then," Ernie said. "What I suggest is this. You take

'is arms and I take 'is legs and we'll swing the little perisher one-two-three as far out as we can into them nice muddy reeds. 'Ow's that?"

"I like it," Raymond said. "And leave 'is 'ands tied together, right?"

"Right," Ernie said. " 'Ow's that with you, snotnose?"

"If that's what you're going to do, I can't very well stop you," Peter said, trying to keep his voice cool and calm.

"Just you try and stop us," Ernie said, grinning, "and then see what 'appens to you."

"One last question," Peter said. "Did you ever take on somebody your own size?"

The moment he said it, he knew he had made a mistake. He saw the flush coming to Ernie's cheeks, and there was a dangerous little spark dancing in his small black eyes.

Luckily, at that very moment, Raymond saved the situation. "Hey! Lookit that bird swimmin' in the reeds over there!" he shouted, pointing. "Let's 'ave 'im!"

It was a mallard drake with a curvy spoon-shaped yellow beak and a head of emerald green with a white ring round its neck. "Now those you really *can* eat," Raymond went on. "It's a wild duck."

"I'll 'ave 'im!" Ernie cried. He let go of the prisoner's arm and lifted the gun to his shoulder.

"This is a bird sanctuary," Peter said.

"A what?" Ernie asked, lowering the gun.

"Nobody shoots birds here. It's strictly forbidden."

" 'Oo says it's forbidden?"

"The owner, Mr. Douglas Highton."

"You must be joking," Ernie said and he raised the gun again. He shot. The duck crumpled in the water.

"Go get 'im," Ernie said to Peter. "Cut 'is 'ands free, Raymond, 'cause then 'ee can be our flippin' gundog and fetch the birds after we shoot 'em."

Raymond took out his knife and cut the string binding the small boy's wrists.

"Go on!" Ernie snapped. "Go get 'im!"

The killing of the beautiful duck had disturbed Peter very much. "I refuse," he said.

Ernie hit him across the face hard with his open hand. Peter didn't fall down, but a small trickle of blood began running out of one nostril.

"You dirty little perisher!" Ernie said. "You just try refusin' me one more time and I'm goin' to make you a promise. And the promise is like this. You refuse me just one more time and I'm goin' to knock out every single one of them shiny white front teeth of yours, top and bottom. You unnerstand that?"

Peter said nothing.

"Answer me!" Ernie barked. "Do you unnerstand that?"

"Yes," Peter said quietly. "I understand."

"Get on with it, then!" Ernie shouted.

Peter walked down the bank, into the muddy water, through the reeds, and picked up the duck. He brought it back, and Raymond took it from him and tied string around its legs.

"Now we got a retriever dog with us, let's see if we can't get us a few more of them ducks," Ernie said. He strolled along the bank, gun in hand, searching the reeds. Suddenly he stopped. He crouched. He put a finger to his lips and said, "Sshh!"

Raymond went over to join him. Peter stood a few yards away his trousers covered with mud up to the knees.

"Lookit in there!" Ernie whispered, pointing into a dense patch of bullrushes. "D'you see what I see?"

"Holy cats!" cried Raymond. "What a beauty!"

Peter, peering from a little farther away into the rushes, saw at once what they were looking at. It was a swan, a

magnificent white swan sitting serenely upon her nest. The
nest itself was a huge pile of reeds and rushes that rose up
about two feet above the waterline, and upon the top of all
this, the swan was sitting like a great white lady of the lake.
Her head was turned toward the boys on the bank, alert and
watchful.

"'Ow about *that?*" Ernie said. "That's better'n ducks,
ain't it?"

"You think you can get 'er?" Raymond asked.

"Of course I can get 'er. I'll drill a 'ole right through 'er
noggin!"

Peter felt a wild rage beginning to build up inside him.
He walked up to the two bigger boys. "I wouldn't shoot that
swan if I were you," he said, trying to keep his voice calm.
"Swans are the most protected birds in England."

"And what's that got to do with it?" Ernie asked him,
sneering.

"And I'll tell you something else," Peter went on, throwing all caution away. "Nobody shoots a bird sitting on its
nest. Absolutely nobody! She may even have cygnets under
her! You just can't do it!"

"'Oo says we can't?" Raymond asked, sneering. "Mister
bleedin' snottynose Peter Watson, is that the one 'oo says
it?"

"The whole country says it," Peter answered. "The law
says it and the police say it and *everyone* says it!"

"*I* don't say it!" Ernie said, raising his gun.

"Don't!" screamed Peter. "Please don't!"

Crack! The gun went off. The bullet hit the swan right in
the middle of her elegant head and the long white neck
collapsed onto the side of the nest.

"Got 'im!" cried Ernie.

"Hot shot!" shouted Raymond.

Ernie turned to Peter, who was standing small and white-faced and absolutely rigid. "Now go get 'im," he ordered.

Once again, Peter didn't move.

Ernie came up close to the smaller boy and bent down and stuck his face right up to Peter's. "I'm tellin' you for the last time," he said soft and dangerous. "Go get 'im!"

Tears were running down Peter's face as he went slowly down the bank and entered the water. He waded out to the dead swan and picked it up tenderly with both hands. Underneath it were two tiny cygnets, their bodies covered with yellow down. They were huddling together in the center of the nest.

"Any eggs?" Ernie shouted from the bank.

"No," Peter answered. "Nothing." There was a chance, he felt, that when the male swan returned, it would continue to feed the young ones on its own if they were left in the nest. He certainly did not want to leave them to the tender mercies of Ernie and Raymond.

Peter carried the dead swan back to the edge of the lake. He placed it on the ground. Then he stood up and faced the two others. His eyes, still wet with tears, were blazing with fury. "That was a filthy thing to do!" he shouted. "It was a stupid, pointless act of vandalism! You're a couple of ignorant idiots! It's you who ought to be dead instead of the swan! You're not fit to be alive!"

He stood there, as tall as he could stand, splendid in his fury, facing the two taller boys and not caring any longer what they did to him.

Ernie didn't hit him this time. He seemed just a tiny bit taken aback at first by this outburst, but he quickly recovered. And now his loose lips formed themselves into a sly wet smirk and his small close-together eyes began to glint in a most malicious manner. "So you like swans, is that right?" he asked softly.

"I like swans and I hate you!" Peter cried.

"And am I right in thinkin'," Ernie went on, still smirking "am I absolutely right in thinkin' that you wished this old swan down 'ere were alive instead of dead?"

"That's a stupid question!" Peter shouted.

" 'Ee needs a clip over the ear-'ole," Raymond said.

"Wait," Ernie said. "I'm doin' this exercise." He turned back to Peter. "So if I could make this swan come alive and go flyin' round the sky all over again, then you'd be 'appy. Right?"

"That's another stupid question!" Peter cried out. "Who d'you think you are?"

"I'll tell you 'oo I am," Ernie said. "I'm a magic man, that's 'oo I am. And just to make you 'appy and contented, I am about to do a magic trick that'll make this dead swan come alive and go flyin' all over the sky once again."

"Rubbish!" Peter said. "I'm going." He turned and started to walk away.

"Grab 'im!" Ernie said.

Raymond grabbed him.

"Leave me alone!" Peter cried out.

Raymond slapped him on the cheek, hard. "Now, now," he said. "Don't fight with auntie, not unless you want to get 'urt."

"Gimme your knife," Ernie said, holding out his hand. Raymond gave him his knife.

Ernie knelt down beside the dead swan and stretched out one of its enormous wings. "Watch this," he said.

"What's the big idea?" Raymond asked.

"Wait and see," Ernie said. And now, using the knife, he proceeded to sever the great white wing from the swan's body. There is a joint in the bone where the wing meets the side of the bird, and Ernie located this and slid the knife into the joint and cut through the tendon. The knife was very sharp and it cut well, and soon the wing came away all in one piece.

Ernie turned the swan over and severed the other wing. "String," he said, holding out his hand to Raymond.

Raymond, who was grasping Peter by the arm, was watching, fascinated. "Where'd you learn 'ow to butcher up a bird like that?" he asked.

"With chickens," Ernie said. "We used to nick chickens from up at Stevens Farm and cut 'em up into chicken parts and sell 'em to a shop in Aylesbury. Gimme the string."

Raymond gave him the ball of string. Ernie cut off six pieces, each about a yard long.

There are a series of strong bones running along the top edge of a swan's wing, and Ernie took one of the wings and started tying one end of the bits of string all the way along the top edge of the great wing. When he had done this, he lifted the wing with the six string-ends dangling from it and said to Peter, "Stick out your arm."

"You're absolutely mad!" the smaller boy shouted. "You're demented!"

"Make 'im stick it out," Ernie said to Raymond.

Raymond held up a clenched fist in front of Peter's face and dabbed it gently against his nose. "You see this," he said. "Well I'm goin' to smash you right in the kisser with it unless you do exactly as you're told, see? Now, stick out your arm, there's a good little boy."

Peter felt his resistance collapsing. He couldn't hold out against these people any longer. For a few seconds, he stared at Ernie. Ernie with the tiny close-together black eyes gave the impression he would be capable of doing just about anything if he got really angry. Ernie, Peter felt at that moment, might quite easily kill a person if he were to lose his temper. Ernie, the dangerous, backward child, was playing games now, and it would be very unwise to spoil his fun. Peter held out an arm.

Ernie then proceeded to tie the six string-ends one by one to Peter's arm, and when he had finished, the white wing of the swan was securely attached along the entire length of the arm itself.

" 'Ow's that, eh?" Ernie said, stepping back and surveying his work.

"Now the other one," Raymond said, catching on to what Ernie was doing. "You can't expect 'im to go flyin' round the sky with only one wing, can you?"

"Second wing comin' up," Ernie said. He knelt down again and tied six more lengths of string to the top bones of the second wing. Then he stood up again. "Let's 'ave the other arm," he said.

Peter, feeling sick and ridiculous, held out his other arm. Ernie strapped the wing tightly along the length of it.

"Now!" Ernie cried, clapping his hands and dancing a little jig on the grass. "Now we got ourselves a real live swan all over again! Didn't I tell you I was a magic man? Didn't I tell you I was goin' to do a magic trick and make this dead swan come alive and go flyin' all over the sky? Didn't I tell you that?"

Peter stood there in the sunshine beside the lake on this beautiful May morning, the enormous limp and slightly bloodied wings dangling grotesquely at his sides. "Have you finished?" he said.

"Swans don't talk," Ernie said. "Keep your flippin' beak shut! And save your energy, laddie, because you're goin' to need all the strength and energy you got when it comes to flyin' round in the sky." Ernie picked up his gun from the ground, then he grabbed Peter by the back of the neck with his free hand and said, "March!"

They marched along the bank of the lake until they came to a tall and graceful willow tree. There they halted. The tree was a weeping willow, and the long branches hung down from a great height and almost touched the surface of the lake.

"And now the magic swan is goin' to show us a bit of magic flyin'," Ernie announced. "So what you're goin' to do, Mister Swan, is to climb up to the very top of this tree, and when you get there you're goin' to spread out your wings like a good clever little swannee-swan-swan and you're goin' to take off!"

"Fantastic!" cried Raymond. "Terrific! I like it very much!"

"So do I," Ernie said. "Because now we're goin' to find out just exactly 'ow clever this clever little swannee-swan-swan really is. 'Ee's terribly clever at school, we all know that, and 'ee's top of the class and everything else that's lovely, but let's see just exactly 'ow clever 'ee is when 'ee's at the top of the tree! Right, Mister Swan?" He gave Peter a push toward the tree.

How much farther could this madness go? Peter wondered. He was beginning to feel a little mad himself, as though nothing was real anymore and none of it was actually happening. But the thought of being high up in the tree and out of reach of these hooligans at last was something that appealed to him greatly. When he was up there, he could stay up there. He doubted very much if they would bother to come up after him. And even if they did, he could surely climb away from them along a thin limb that would not take the weight of two people.

The tree was a fairly easy one to climb, with several low branches to give him a start up. He began climbing. The huge white wings dangling from his arms kept getting in the way, but it didn't matter. What mattered now to Peter was that every inch upward was another inch away from his tormentors below. He had never been a great one for tree climbing and he wasn't especially good at it, but nothing in the world was going to stop him from getting to the top of this one. And once he was there, he thought it unlikely they would even be able to see him because of the leaves.

"Higher!" shouted Ernie's voice. "Keep goin'!"

Peter kept going, and eventually he arrived at a point where it was impossible to go higher. His feet were now standing on a branch that was about as thick as a person's wrist, and this particular branch reached far out over the lake and then curved gracefully downward. All the branches above him were very thin and whippy, but the one he was holding onto with his hands was quite strong enough for the purpose. He stood there, resting after the climb. He looked down for the first time. He was very high up, at least fifty feet. But he couldn't see the boys. They were no longer standing at the base of the tree. Was it possible they had gone away at last?

"All right, Mister Swan!" came the dreaded voice of Ernie. "Now listen carefully!"

The two of them had walked some distance away from the tree to a point where they had a clear view of the small boy at the top. Looking down at them now, Peter realized how very sparse and slender the leaves of a willow tree were. They gave him almost no cover at all.

"Listen carefully, Mister Swan!" the voice was shouting. "Start walking out along that branch you're standin' on! Keep goin' till you're right over the nice muddy water! Then you take off!"

Peter didn't move. He was fifty feet above them now and they weren't ever going to reach him again. From down below, there was a long silence. It lasted maybe half a minute. He kept his eyes on the two distant figures in the field. They were standing quite still, looking up at him.

"All right then, Mister Swan!" came Ernie's voice again. "I'm gonna count to ten, right? And if you ain't spread them wings and flown away by then, I'm gonna shoot you down instead with this little gun! And that'll make two swans I've knocked off today instead of one! So here we go, Mister Swan! One!... Two!... Three!... Four!... Five! ... Six!..."

Peter remained still. Nothing would make him move from now on.

"Seven!... Eight!... Nine!... Ten!"

Peter saw the gun coming up to the shoulder. It was pointing straight at him. Then he heard the *crack* of the rifle and the *zip* of the bullet as it whistled past his head. It was a frightening thing. But he still didn't move. He could see Ernie loading the gun with another bullet.

"Last chance!" yelled Ernie. "The next one's gonna get you!"

Peter stayed put. He waited. He watched the boy who was standing among the buttercups in the meadow far below with the other boy beside him. The gun came up once again to the shoulder.

This time he heard the *crack* and at the same instant the bullet hit him in the thigh. There was no pain, but the force of it was devastating. It was as though someone had whacked him on the leg with a sledgehammer, and it knocked both feet off the branch he was standing on. He scrabbled with his hands to hang on. The small branch he was holding onto bent over and split.

Some people, when they have taken too much and have been driven beyond the point of endurance, simply crumple and give up. There are others, though they are not many, who will for some reason always be unconquerable. You meet them in time of war and also in time of peace. They have an indomitable spirit and nothing, neither pain nor torture nor threat of death, will cause them to give up.

Little Peter Watson was one of these. And as he fought and scrabbled to prevent himself from falling out of the top of that tree, it came to him suddenly that he was going to win. He looked up and he saw a light shining over the waters of the lake that was of such brilliance and beauty he was unable to look away from it. The light was beckoning him, drawing him on, and he dived toward the light and spread his wings.

Three different people reported seeing a great white swan circling over the village that morning, a schoolteacher called Emily Mead, a man who was replacing some tiles on the roof of the chemist's shop whose name was William Eyles, and a boy called John Underwood who was flying his model airplane in a nearby field.

And that morning, Mrs. Watson, who was washing up some dishes in her kitchen sink, happened to glance up through the window at the exact moment when something huge and white came flopping down onto the lawn in her back garden. She rushed outside. She went down on her knees beside the small crumpled figure of her only son. "Oh, my darling!" she cried, near to hysterics and hardly believing what she saw. "My darling boy! What happened to you?"

"My leg hurts," Peter said, opening his eyes. Then he fainted.

"It's bleeding!" she cried, and she picked him up and carried him inside. Quickly she phoned for the doctor and the ambulance. And while she was waiting for help to come, she fetched a pair of scissors and began cutting the string that held the two great wings of the swan to her son's arms.

The Wonderful Story
of Henry Sugar

1

Henry Sugar was forty-one years old and unmarried. He was also wealthy.

He was wealthy because he had had a rich father, who was now dead. He was unmarried because he was too selfish to share any of his money with a wife.

He was six feet two inches tall, but he wasn't really as good-looking as he thought he was.

He paid a great deal of attention to his clothes. He went to an expensive tailor for his suits, to a shirtmaker for his shirts, and to a bootmaker for his shoes.

He used a costly aftershave on his face, and he kept his hands soft with a cream that contained turtle oil.

His hairdresser trimmed his hair once every ten days, and he always took a manicure at the same time.

His upper front teeth had been capped at incredible expense because the originals had had a rather nasty yellowish tinge. A small mole had been removed from his left cheek by a plastic surgeon.

He drove a Ferrari car that must have cost him about the same as a country cottage.

He lived in London in the summer, but as soon as the first frosts appeared in October, he was off to the West Indies or the South of France, where he stayed with friends. All his friends were wealthy from inherited money.

Henry had never done a day's work in his life, and his personal motto, which he had invented himself, was this: *It is better to incur a mild rebuke than to perform an onerous task.* His friends thought this was hilarious.

Men like Henry Sugar are to be found drifting like seaweed all over the world. They can be seen especially in London, New York, Paris, Nassau, Montego Bay, Cannes and St. Tropez. They are not particularly bad men. But they are not good men either. They are of no real importance. They are simply a part of the decoration.

All of them, all wealthy people of this type, have one peculiarity in common: they have a terrific urge to make themselves still wealthier than they already are. The million is never enough. Nor is the two million. Always, they have this insatiable longing to get more money. And that is because they live in constant terror of waking up one morning and finding there's nothing in the bank.

These people all employ the same methods for trying to increase their fortunes. They buy stocks and shares, and watch them going up and down. They play roulette and blackjack for high stakes in casinos. They bet on horses. They bet on just about everything. Henry Sugar had once staked a thousand pounds on the result of a tortoise race on Lord Liverpool's tennis lawn. And he had wagered double that sum with a man called Esmond Hanbury on an even sillier bet, which was as follows: They let Henry's dog out into the garden and watched it through the window. But before the dog was let out, each man had to guess beforehand what would be the first object the dog would lift its leg against. Would it be a wall, a post, a bush or a tree? Esmond chose a wall. Henry, who had been studying his dog's habits for days with a view to making this particular bet, chose a tree, and he won the money.

With ridiculous games such as these did Henry and his friends try to conquer the deadly boredom of being both idle and wealthy.

Henry himself, as you may have noticed, was not above cheating a little on these friends of his if he saw the chance. The bet with the dog was definitely not honest. Nor, if you want to know, was the bet on the tortoise race. Henry cheated on that one by secretly forcing a little sleeping-pill powder into the mouth of his opponent's tortoise an hour before the race.

And now that you've got a rough idea of the sort of person Henry Sugar was, I can begin my story.

One summer weekend, Henry drove down from London to Guildford to stay with Sir William Wyndham. The house was magnificent, and so were the grounds, but when Henry arrived on that Saturday afternoon, it was already pelting with rain. Tennis was out, croquet was out. So was swimming in Sir William's outdoor pool. The host and his guests sat glumly in the drawing room, staring at the rain splashing against the windows. The very rich are enormously resentful of bad weather. It is the one discomfort that their money cannot do anything about.

Somebody in the room said, "Let's have a game of canasta for lovely high stakes."

The others thought that a splendid idea, but as there were five people in all, one would have to sit out. They cut the cards. Henry drew the lowest, the unlucky card.

The other four sat down and began to play. Henry was annoyed at being out of the game. He wandered out of the drawing room into the great hall. He stared at the pictures for a few moments, then he walked on through the house, bored to death and having nothing to do. Finally, he mooched into the library.

Sir William's father had been a famous book collector, and all four walls of this huge room were lined with books from floor to ceiling. Henry Sugar was not impressed. He wasn't even interested. The only books he read were detective novels and thrillers. He ambled aimlessly round the room, looking to see if he could find any of the sort of books he liked. But the ones in Sir William's library were

all leather-bound volumes with names on them like Balzac,
Ibsen, Voltaire, Johnson and Pepys. Boring rubbish, the
whole lot of it, Henry told himself. And he was just about
to leave when his eye was caught and held by a book that was
quite different from all the others. It was so slim he would
never have noticed it if it hadn't been sticking out a little
from the ones on either side. And when he pulled it from
the shelf, he saw that it was actually nothing more than a
cardboard-covered exercise book of the kind children use at
school. The cover was dark blue, but there was nothing
written on it. Henry opened the exercise book. On the first
page, handprinted in ink, it said:

A REPORT ON AN INTERVIEW WITH IMHRAT KHAN,
THE MAN WHO COULD SEE WITHOUT HIS EYES
BY JOHN F. CARTWRIGHT, M.D.
BOMBAY, INDIA   DECEMBER 1934

That sounds mildly interesting, Henry told himself. He
turned over a page. What followed was all handwritten in
black ink. The writing was clear and neat. Henry read the
first two pages standing up. Suddenly, he found himself want-
ing to read on. This was good stuff. It was fascinating. He
carried the little book over to a leather armchair by the
window and settled himself comfortably. Then he started
reading again from the beginning.

2

This is what Henry read in the little blue exercise book:
I, John Cartwright, am a surgeon at Bombay General
Hospital. On the morning of the second of December, 1934,
I was in the doctors' rest room having a cup of tea. There
were three other doctors there with me, all having a well-

earned tea break. They were Dr. Marshall, Dr. Phillips and Dr. Macfarlane. There was a knock on the door. "Come in," I said.

The door opened and an Indian came in who smiled at us and said, "Excuse me, please. Could I ask you gentlemen a favor?"

The doctors' rest room was a most private place. Nobody other than a doctor was allowed to enter it except in an emergency.

"This is a private room," Dr. Macfarlane said sharply.

"Yes, yes," he answered. "I know that and I am very sorry to be bursting in like this, sirs, but I have a most interesting thing to show you."

All four of us were pretty annoyed and we didn't say anything.

"Gentlemen," he said. "I am a man who can see without using his eyes."

We still didn't invite him to go on. But we didn't kick him out either.

"You can cover my eyes in any way you wish," he said. "You can bandage my head with fifty bandages and I will still be able to read you a book."

He seemed perfectly serious. I felt my curiosity beginning to stir. "Come here," I said. He came over to me. "Turn around." He turned around. I placed my hands firmly over his eyes, holding the lids closed. "Now," I said, "one of the other doctors in the room is going to hold up some fingers. Tell me how many he's holding up."

Dr. Marshall held up seven fingers.

"Seven," the Indian said.

"Once more," I said.

Dr. Marshall clenched both fists and hid all his fingers.

"No fingers," the Indian said.

I removed my hands from his eyes. "Not bad," I said.

"Hold on," Dr. Marshall said. "Let's try this." There was a doctor's white coat hanging from a peg on the door. Dr. Marshall took it down and rolled in into a sort of long scarf. He then wound it around the Indian's head and held the ends tight at the back. "Try him now," Dr. Marshall said.

I took a key from my pocket. "What is this?" I asked.

"A key," he answered.

I put the key back and held up an empty hand. "What is this object?" I asked him.

"There isn't any object," the Indian said. "Your hand is empty."

Dr. Marshall removed the covering from the man's eyes. "How do you do it?" he asked. "What's the trick?"

"There is no trick," the Indian said. "It is a genuine thing that I have managed after years of training."

"What sort of training?" I asked.

"Forgive me, sir," he said, "but that is a private matter."

"Then why did you come here?" I asked.

"I came to request a favor of you," he said.

The Indian was a tall man of about thirty with light brown skin the color of a coconut. He had a small black moustache. Also, there was a curious matting of black hair growing all over the outsides of his ears. He wore a white cotton robe, and he had sandals on his bare feet.

"You see, gentlemen," he went on. "I am at present earning my living by working in a traveling theater, and we have just arrived here in Bombay. Tonight we give our opening performance."

"Where do you give it?" I asked.

"In the Royal Palace Hall," he answered. "In Acacia Street. I am the star performer. I am billed on the program as 'Imhrat Khan, the man who sees without his eyes.' And it is my duty to advertise the show in a big way. If we don't sell tickets, we don't eat."

"What does this have to do with us?" I asked him.

"Very interesting for you," he said. "Lots of fun. Let me explain. You see, whenever our theater arrives in a new town, I myself go straight to the largest hospital and I ask the doctors there to bandage my eyes. I ask them to do it in the most expert fashion. They must make sure my eyes are completely covered many times over. It is important that this job is done by doctors, otherwise people will think I am cheating. Then, when I am fully bandaged, I go out into the street and I do a dangerous thing."

"What do you mean by that?" I asked.

"What I mean is that I do something that is extremely dangerous for someone who cannot see."

"What do you do?" I asked.

"It is very interesting," he said. "And you will see me do it if you will be so kind as to bandage me up first. It would be a great favor to me if you will do this little thing, sirs."

I looked at the other three doctors. Dr. Phillips said he had to go back to his patients. Dr. Macfarlane said the same. Dr. Marshall said, "Well, why not? It might be amusing. It won't take a minute."

"I'm with you," I said. "But let's do the job properly. Let's make absolutely sure he can't peep."

"You are extremely kind," the Indian said. "Please do whatever you wish."

Dr. Phillips and Dr. Macfarlane left the room.

"Before we bandage him," I said to Dr. Marshall, "let's first of all seal down his eyelids. When we've done that, we'll fill his eye sockets with something soft and solid and sticky."

"Such as what?" Dr. Marshall asked.

"What about dough?"

"Dough would be perfect," Dr. Marshall said.

"Right," I said. "If you will nip down to the hospital bakery and get some dough, I'll take him into the surgery and seal his lids."

I led the Indian out of the rest room and down the long hospital corridor to the surgery. "Lie down there," I said, indicating the high bed. He lay down. I took a small bottle from the cupboard. It had an eyedropper in the top. "This is something called colodion," I told him. "It will harden over your closed eyelids so that it is impossible for you to open them."

"How do I get it off afterward?" he asked me.

"Alcohol will dissolve it away quite easily," I said. "It's perfectly harmless. Close your eyes now."

The Indian closed his eyes. I applied colodion to both lids. "Keep them closed," I said. "Wait for it to harden."

In a couple of minutes, the colodion had made a hard film over the eyelids, sticking them down tight. "Try to open them," I said.

He tried but couldn't.

Dr. Marshall came in with a basin of dough. It was the ordinary white dough used for baking bread. It was nice and soft. I took a lump of the dough and plastered it over one of the Indian's eyes. I filled the whole socket and let the dough overlap onto the surrounding skin. Then I pressed the edges down hard. I did the same with the other eye.

"That isn't too uncomfortable, is it?" I asked.

"No," the Indian said. "It's fine."

"You do the bandaging," I said to Dr. Marshall. "My fingers are too sticky."

"A pleasure," Dr. Marshall said. "Watch this." He took a thick wad of cotton wool and laid it on top of the Indian's dough-filled eyes. The cotton-wool stuck to the dough and stayed in place. "Sit down, please," Dr. Marshall said.

The Indian sat on the bed.

Dr. Marshall took a roll of three-inch bandage and proceeded to wrap it round and round the man's head. The bandage held the cotton wool and the dough firmly in place. Dr. Marshall pinned the bandage. After that, he took a second bandage and began to wrap that one not only around the man's eyes but around his entire face and head.

"Please to leave my nose free for breathing," the Indian said.

"Of course," Dr. Marshall answered. He finished the job and pinned down the end of the bandage. "How's that?" he asked.

"Splendid," I said. "There's no way he can possibly see through that."

The whole of the Indian's head was now swathed in thick white bandage, and the only thing you could see was the end of the nose sticking out. He looked like a man who had had some terrible brain operation.

"How does that feel?" Dr. Marshall asked him.

"It feels good," the Indian said. "I must compliment you gentlemen on doing such a fine job."

"Off you go, then," Dr. Marshall said, grinning at me. "Show us how clever you are at seeing things now."

The Indian got off the bed and walked straight to the door. He opened the door and went out.

"Great Scott!" I said. "Did you see that? He put his hand right on the doorknob!"

Dr. Marshall had stopped grinning. His face had suddenly gone white. "I'm going after him," he said, rushing for the door. I rushed for the door as well.

The Indian was walking quite normally along the hospital corridor. Dr. Marshall and I were about five yards behind him. And very spooky it was to watch this man with the enormous white and totally bandaged head strolling casually along the corridor just like anyone else. It was especially spooky when you knew for a certainty that his eyelids were sealed, that his eye sockets were filled with dough, and that there was a great wad of cotton wool and bandages on top of that.

I saw a native orderly coming along the corridor toward the Indian. He was pushing a food trolley. Suddenly the orderly caught sight of the man with the white head, and he froze. The bandaged Indian stepped casually to one side of the trolley and went on.

"He saw it!" I cried. "He must have seen that trolley! He walked right round it! This is absolutely unbelievable!"

Dr. Marshall didn't answer me. His cheeks were white, his whole face rigid with shocked disbelief.

The Indian came to the stairs and started to go down them. He went down with no trouble at all. He didn't even put a hand on the handrail. Several people were coming up the stairs. Each of them stopped, gasped, stared and quickly got out of the way.

At the bottom of the stairs, the Indian turned right and headed for the doors that led out into the street. Dr. Marshall and I kept close behind him.

The entrance to our hospital stands back a little from the street, and there is a rather grand series of steps leading down from the entrance into a small courtyard with acacia trees around it. Dr. Marshall and I came out into the blazing sunshine and stood at the top of the steps. Below us, in the courtyard, we saw a crowd of maybe a hundred people. At least half of them were barefoot children, and as our white-headed Indian walked down the steps, they all cheered and shouted and surged toward him. He greeted them by holding both hands above his head.

Suddenly I saw the bicycle. It was over to one side at the bottom of the steps, and a small boy was holding it. The bicycle itself was quite ordinary, but on the back of it, fixed somehow to the rear wheel frame, was a huge placard, about five feet square. On the placard were written the following words:

Imhrat Khan, The Man Who Sees Without His Eyes!
Today my eyes have been bandaged by hospital doctors!
Appearing Tonight and all this week at
The Royal Palace Hall, Acacia Street, at 7 P.M.
Don't miss it! You will see miracles performed!

Our Indian had reached the bottom of the steps and now he walked straight over to the bicycle. He said something to the boy, and the boy smiled. The Indian mounted the bicycle. The crowd made way for him. Then, lo and behold, this fellow with the blocked-up bandaged eyes now proceeded to ride across the courtyard and straight out into the bustling honking traffic of the street beyond! The crowd cheered louder than ever. The barefoot children ran after him, squealing and laughing. For a minute or so, we were able to keep him in sight. We saw him riding superbly down the busy street with cars whizzing past him and a bunch of children running in his wake. Then he turned a corner and was gone.

"I feel quite giddy," Dr. Marshall said. "I can't bring myself to believe it."

"We have to believe it," I said. "He couldn't possibly have removed the dough from under the bandages. We never let him out of our sight. And as for unsealing his eyelids, that job would take him five minutes with cotton wool and alcohol."

"Do you know what I think," Dr. Marshall said. "I think we have witnessed a miracle."

We turned and walked slowly back into the hospital.

3

For the rest of the day, I was kept busy with patients in the hospital. At six in the evening, I came off duty and drove back to my flat for a shower and a change of clothes. It was the hottest time of year in Bombay, and even after sundown the heat was like an open furnace. If you sat still in a chair and did nothing, the sweat would come seeping out of your skin. Your face glistened with dampness all day long and your shirt stuck to your chest. I took a long cool shower. I drank a whiskey and soda sitting on the veranda, with only a towel around my waist. Then I put on some clean clothes.

At ten minutes to seven, I was outside the Royal Palace Hall in Acacia Street. It was not much of a place. It was one of those smallish seedy halls that can be hired inexpensively for meetings or dances. There was a fair-sized crowd of local Indians milling around outside the ticket office, and a large poster over the entrance proclaimed that THE INTERNATIONAL THEATER COMPANY was performing every night that week. It said there would be jugglers and conjurors and acrobats and sword swallowers and fire eaters and snake charmers and a one-act play entitled *The Rajah and the Tiger Lady*. But above all this and in by far the largest letters, it said IMHRAT KHAN, THE MIRACLE MAN WHO SEES WITHOUT HIS EYES.

I bought a ticket and went in.

The show lasted two hours. To my surprise, I thoroughly enjoyed it. All the performers were excellent. I liked the man who juggled with cooking utensils. He had a saucepan, a frying pan, a baking tray, a huge plate and a casserole pot all flying through the air at the same time. The snake charmer had a big green snake that stood almost on the tip of its tail and swayed to the music of his flute. The fire eater ate fire and the sword swallower pushed a thin-pointed rapier at least four feet down his throat and into his stomach. Last of all, to a great fanfare of trumpets, our friend Imhrat Khan came on to do his act. The bandages we had put on him at the hospital had now been removed.

Members of the audience were called onto the stage to

blindfold him with sheets and scarves and turbans, and in the end there was so much material wrapped around his head he could hardly keep his balance. He was then given a revolver. A small boy came out and stood at the left of the stage. I recognized him as the one who had held the bicycle outside the hospital that morning. The boy placed a tin can on the top of his head and stood quite still. The audience became deathly silent as Imhrat Khan took aim. He fired. The bang made us all jump. The tin can flew off the boy's head and clattered to the floor. The boy picked it up and showed the bullet hole to the audience. Everyone clapped and cheered. The boy smiled.

Then the boy stood against a wooden screen and Imhrat Khan threw knives all around his body, most of them going very close indeed. This was a splendid act. Not many people could have thrown knives with such accuracy even with their eyes uncovered, but here he was, this extraordinary fellow, with his head so swathed in sheets it looked like a great snowball on a stick, and he was flicking the sharp knives into the screen within a hairsbreadth of the boy's head. The boy smiled all the way through the act, and when it was over the audience stamped its feet and screamed with excitement.

Imhrat Khan's last act, though not so spectacular, was even more impressive. A metal barrel was brought on stage. The audience was invited to examine it, to make sure there were no holes. There were no holes. The barrel was then placed over Imhrat Khan's already bandaged head. It came down over his shoulders and as far as his elbows, pinning the upper part of his arms to his sides. But he could still hold out his forearms and his hands. Someone put a needle in one of his hands and a length of cotton thread in the other. With no false moves, he neatly threaded the cotton through the eye of the needle. I was flabbergasted.

As soon as the show was over, I made my way backstage.

I found Imhrat Khan in a small but clean dressing room, sitting quietly on a wooden stool. The little Indian boy was unwinding the mass of scarves and sheets from around his head.

"Ah," he said. "It is my friend the doctor from the hospital. Come in, sir, come in."

"I saw the show," I said.

"And what did you think?"

"I liked it very much. I thought you were wonderful."

"Thank you," he said. "That is a high compliment."

"I must congratulate your assistant as well," I said, nodding to the small boy. "He is very brave."

"He cannot speak English," the Indian said. "But I will tell him what you said." He spoke rapidly to the boy in Hindustani, and the boy nodded solemnly but said nothing.

"Look," I said. "I did you a small favor this morning. Would you do me one in return? Would you consent to come out and have supper with me?"

All the wrappings were off his head now. He smiled at me and said, "I think you are feeling curious, doctor. Am I not right?"

"Very curious," I said. "I'd like to talk to you."

Once again, I was struck by the peculiarly thick matting of black hair growing on the outsides of his ears. I had not seen anything quite like it on another person. "I have never been questioned by a doctor before," he said. "But I have no objection. It would be a pleasure to have supper with you."

"Shall I wait in the car?"

"Yes, please," he said. "I must wash myself and get out of these dirty clothes."

I told him what my car looked like and said I would be waiting outside.

He emerged fifteen minutes later, wearing a clean white

cotton robe and the usual sandals on his bare feet. And soon the two of us were sitting comfortably in a small restaurant that I sometimes went to because it made the best curry in the city. I drank beer with my curry. Imhrat Khan drank lemonade.

"I am not a writer," I said to him, "I am a doctor. But if you will tell me your story from the beginning, if you will explain to me how you developed this magical power of being able to see without your eyes, I will write it down as faithfully as I can. And then, perhaps, I can get it published in the *British Medical Journal* or even in some famous magazine. And because I *am* a doctor and not just some writer trying to sell a story for money, people will be far more inclined to take seriously what I say. It would help you, wouldn't it, to become better known?"

"It would help me very much," he said. "But why should you want to do this?"

"Because I am madly curious," I answered. "That is the only reason."

Imhrat Khan took a mouthful of curried rice and chewed it slowly. Then he said, "Very well, my friend. I will do it."

"Splendid!" I cried. "Let's go back to my flat as soon as we've finished eating and then we can talk without anyone disturbing us."

We finished our meal. I paid the bill. Then I drove Imhrat Khan back to my flat.

4

In the living room, I got out paper and pencils so that I could make notes. I have a sort of private shorthand of my own that I use for taking down the medical history of patients, and with it I am able to record most of what a person says if he doesn't speak too quickly. I think I got just about everything Imhrat Khan said to me that evening, word for word, and here it is. I give it to you exactly as he spoke it:

"I am an Indian, a Hindu," said Imhrat Khan, "and I was born in Akhnur, in Kashmir State, in 1905. My family is poor and my father worked as a ticket inspector on the railway. When I was a small boy of thirteen, an Indian conjuror comes to our school and gives a performance. His name, I remember, is Professor Moor—all conjurors in India call themselves 'professor'—and his tricks are very good. I am tremendously impressed. I think it is real magic. I feel—how shall I call it—I feel a powerful wish to learn about this magic myself, so two days later I run away from home determined to find and to follow my new hero, Professor Moor. I take all my savings, fourteen rupees, and only the clothes I am wearing. I am wearing a white dhoti and sandals. This is 1918 and I am thirteen years old.

"I find out that Professor Moor has gone to Lahore, two hundred miles away, so all alone, I take a ticket, third class, and I get on the train and follow him. In Lahore, I discover the Professor. He is working at his conjuring in a very cheap-type show. I tell him of my admiration and offer myself to him as assistant. He accepts me. My pay? Ah yes, my pay is eight annas a day.

"The Professor teaches me to do the linking-rings trick and my job is to stand in the street before the theater dressed in funny clothes doing the linking rings and calling to the people to come in and see the show.

"For six whole weeks this is very fine. It is much better than going to school. But then what a terrible bombshell I receive when suddenly it comes to me that there is no real magic in Professor Moor, that all is trickery and quickness of the hand. Immediately the Professor is no longer my hero. I lose every bit of interest in my job, but at the same time my whole mind becomes filled with a very strong long-

ing. I long above all things to find out about the real magic
and to discover something about the strange power which is
called yoga.

"To do this, I must find a yogi who is willing to let me
become his disciple. This is not going to be easy. True yogis
do not grow on trees. There are very few of them in the
whole of India. Also, they are fanatically religious people.
Therefore, if I am to have success in finding a teacher, I too
would have to pretend to be a very religious man.

"No, I am actually not religious. And because of that, I
am what you would call a bit of a cheat. I wanted to
acquire yoga powers purely for selfish reasons. I wanted to
use these powers to get fame and fortune.

"Now this was something the true yogi would despise
more than anything in the world. In fact, the true yogi
believes that any yogi who misuses his powers will die an
early and sudden death. A yogi must never perform in public. He must practice his art only in absolute privacy and as
a religious service, otherwise he will be smitten to death.
This I did not believe and I still don't.

"So now my search for a yogi instructor begins. I leave
Professor Moor and go to a town called Amritsar in the
Punjab, where I join a traveling theater company. I have to
make a living while I am searching for the secret, and already I have had success in amateur acting at my school.
So for three years I travel with this theater group all over
the Punjab and by the end of it, when I am sixteen and a
half years old, I am playing top of the bill. All the time I
am saving money and now I have altogether a very great
sum, two thousand rupees.

"It is at that moment that I hear news of a man called
Banerjee. This Banerjee, it is said, is one of the truly great
yogis of India, and he possesses extraordinary yoga powers.
Above all, people are telling of how he has acquired the rare

power of levitation, so that when he prays his whole body leaves the ground and becomes suspended in the air eighteen inches from the soil.

"Ah-ha, I think. This surely is the man for me. This Banerjee is the one that I must seek. So at once I take my savings and leave the theater company and make my way to Rikhikesh, on the banks of the Ganges, where rumor says that Banerjee is living.

"For six months I search for Banerjee. Where is he? Where? Where is Banerjee? Ah yes, they say in Rikhikesh, Banerjee has certainly been in town, but that is a while ago, and even then no one saw him. And now? Now Banerjee has gone to another place. What other place? Ah well, they say, how can one know that. How indeed? How can one know about the movements of such a one as Banerjee. Does he not live a life of absolute seclusion? Does he not? And I say yes. Yes, yes, yes. Of course. That is obvious. Even to me.

"I spend all my savings trying to find this Banerjee, all except thirty-five rupees. But it is no good. However, I stay in Rikhikesh and make a living by doing ordinary conjuring tricks for small groups and suchlike. These are the tricks I have learned from Professor Moor and by nature my sleight of hand is very good.

"Then one day, there I am sitting in the small hotel in Rikhikesh and again I hear talk of the yogi Banerjee. A traveler is saying how he has heard that Banerjee is now living in the jungle, not so very far away, but in the dense jungle and all alone.

"But where?"

"The traveler is not sure where. Possibly, he says, it is over there, in that direction, north of the town, and he points with his finger.

"Well, that is enough for me. I go to the market and begin to bargain for hiring a tonga, which is a horse and cart, and the transaction is just being completed with the driver when up comes a man who has been standing listening nearby and he says that he too is going in that direction. He asks can he come part of the way with me and share the cost. I answer, 'delighted, of course,' and off we go, the man and me sitting in the cart, and the driver driving the horse. Off we go along a very small path which leads right through the jungle.

"And then what truly fantastic luck should happen! I am talking to my companion and I find that he is a disciple of none other than the great Banerjee himself and that he is going now on a visit to his master. So straight out I tell him that I too would like to become a disciple of the yogi.

"He turns and looks at me long and slow, and for perhaps three minutes he does not speak. Then he says, quietly, 'No, that is impossible.'

"All right, I say to myself, we shall see. Then I ask if it is really true that Banerjee levitates when he prays.

" 'Yes,' he says. 'That is true. But no one is allowed to observe the thing happening. No one is ever allowed to come near Banerjee when he is praying.'

"So we go on a little farther in the tonga, talking all the time about Banerjee, and I manage by very careful casual questioning to find out a number of small things about him, such as what time of day he commences with his praying. Then soon the man says, 'I will leave you here. This is where I dismount.'

"I drop him off and I pretend to drive on along my journey, but around a corner I tell the driver to stop and wait. Quickly I jump down and I sneak back along the road, looking for this man, the disciple of Banerjee. He is not on the road. Already he has disappeared into the jungle. But which way? Which side of the road? I stand very still and listen.

"I hear a sort of rustling in the undergrowth. That must be him, I tell myself. If it is not him, then it is a tiger. But it is him. I see him ahead. He is going forward through thick jungle. There is not even a little path where he is walking, and he is having to push his way between tall bamboos and every kind of heavy vegetation. I creep after him. I keep about one hundred yards behind him because I am frightened he may hear me. I can certainly hear him. It is impossible to proceed in silence through very thick jungle, and when I lose sight of him, which is most of the time, I am able to follow his sound.

"For about half an hour this tense game of follow-the-leader goes on. Then suddenly, I can no longer hear the man in front of me. I stop and listen. The jungle is silent. I am terrified that I may have lost him. I creep on a little way, and all at once, through the thick undergrowth, I see before me a little clearing, and in the middle of the clearing are two huts. They are small huts built entirely of jungle leaves and branches. My heart jumps and I feel a great surging of excitement inside me because this, I know for certain, is the place of Banerjee, the yogi.

"The disciple has already disappeared. He must have gone into one of the huts. All is quiet. So now I proceed to make a most careful inspection of the trees and bushes and other things all around. There is a small waterhole beside the nearest hut, and I see a prayer mat beside it, and that, I say to myself, is where Banerjee meditates and prays. Close to this waterhole, not thirty yards away, there is a large tree, a great spreading baobab tree with beautiful thick branches which spread in such a way you can put a bed on them and lie on the bed and still not be seen from underneath. That will be my tree, I say to myself. I shall hide in that tree and wait until Banerjee comes out to pray. Then I will be able to see everything.

"But the disciple has told me that the time of prayer is not until five or six in the evening, so I have several hours to wait. Therefore I at once walk back through the jungle to the road and I speak to the tonga driver. I tell him he too must wait. For this, I have to pay him extra money, but it doesn't matter because now I am so excited I don't care about anything for the moment, not even money.

"And all through the great noontime heat of the jungle I wait beside the tonga, and on through the heavy wet heat of the afternoon, and then, as five o'clock approaches, I make my way quietly back through the jungle to the hut, my heart beating so I can feel it shaking my whole body. I climb up my tree and I hide among the leaves in such a way that I can see but cannot be seen. And I wait. I wait for forty-five minutes.

"A watch? Yes, I have on a wristwatch. I remember it clearly. It was a watch I won in a raffle and I was proud to own it. On the face of my watch it said the maker's name, The Islamia Watch Company, Ludhiana. And so with my watch I am careful to be timing everything that goes on because I want to get every single detail of this experience.

"I sit up in the tree, waiting.

"Then, all at once, a man is coming out of the hut. The man is tall and thin. He is dressed in an orange-colored dhoti and he carries before him a tray with brass pots and incense burners. He goes over and sits down cross-legged on the mat by the waterhole, putting the tray on the ground before him, and all the movements that he makes seem somehow very calm and gentle. He leans forward and scoops a handful of water from the pool and throws it over his shoulder. He takes the incense burner and passes it back and forth across his chest, slowly, in a gentle, flowing manner. He puts his hands palm downward on his knees. He pauses. He takes a long breath through his nostrils. I can see him take a long breath and suddenly I can see his face is changing. There is a sort of brightness coming over all his face, a sort of . . . .well, a sort of brightness on his skin and I can see his face is changing.

"For fourteen minutes he remains quite still in that position, and then, as I look at him, I see, quite positively I see his body lifting slowly . . . slowly . . . slowly off the ground. He is still sitting cross-legged, the hands palm downward on the knees, and his whole body is lifting slowly off the ground, up into the air. Now I can see daylight underneath him. Twelve inches above the ground he is sitting . . . . fifteen inches . . . eighteen . . . twenty . . . and soon he is at least two feet above the prayer mat.

"I stay quite still up there in the tree, watching, and I keep saying to myself, now look carefully, make sure, be certain that you are seeing correctly. There before you, thirty yards away, is a man sitting in great serenity upon the air. Are you seeing him? Yes, I am seeing him. But are you sure there is no illusion? Are you sure there is no deception? Are you sure you are not imagining? Are you sure? Yes, I am sure, I say. I am sure. I stare at him marveling. For a long while I keep staring, and then the body is coming slowly down again toward the earth. I see it coming. I see it moving gently downward, slowly downward, lowering to the earth until again his buttocks rest upon the mat.

"Forty-six minutes by my watch it had been suspended! I timed it.

"And then, for a long, long while, for over two hours, the man remains sitting absolutely still, like a stone person, with not the slightest movement. To me, it does not seem that he is breathing. His eyes are closed, and still there is this brightness on his face and also this slightly smiling look, a thing I have not seen on any other face in all my life since then.

"At last he stirs. He moves his hands. He stands up. He bends down again. He picks up the tray and goes slowly back into the hut. I am wonderstruck. I feel exalted. I forget all caution and I climb down quickly from the tree and run straight over to the hut and rush in through the door. Banerjee is bending over, washing his feet and hands in a basin. His back is toward me, but he hears me and he turns quickly and straightens up. There is great surprise on his face and the first thing he says is, 'How long have you been here?' He says it sharply, like he is not pleased.

"At once I tell the whole truth, the whole story about being up in the tree and watching him, and at the end I tell him there is nothing I want in life except to become his disciple. Please will he let me become his disciple?

"Suddenly he seems to explode. He becomes furious and he begins shouting at me. 'Get out!' he shouts. 'Get out of here! Get out! Get out! Get out!' And in his fury he picks up a small brick and flings it at me and it strikes my right leg just below the knee and tears the flesh. I have the scar still. I will show it to you. There, you see, just below the knee.

"Banerjee's anger is terrible and I am very frightened. I turn and run away. I run back through the jungle to where the tonga driver is waiting, and we drive home to Rikhis-kesh. But that night I regain my courage. I make for myself a decision and it is this: that I will return every day to the hut of Banerjee, and I will keep on and on at him until at last he *has* to take me on as a disciple, just to get himself some peace.

"This I do. Each day I go to see him and each day his anger pours out upon me like a volcano, him shouting and yelling and me standing there frightened but also obstinate and repeating always to him my wish to become a disciple. For five days it is like this. Then, all at once, on my sixth visit, Banerjee seems to become quite calm, quite polite. He explains he cannot himself take me on as a disciple. But he will give me a note, he says, to another man, a friend, a great yogi, who lives in Hardawar. I am to go there and I will receive help and instruction."

5

Imhrat Khan paused and asked me if he might have a glass of water. I fetched it for him. He took a long, slow drink, then he went on with his story:

"This is in 1922 and I am nearly seventeen years old. So I go to Hardawar. And there I find the yogi, and because I have a letter from the great Banerjee, he consents to give me instruction.

"Now what is this instruction?

"It is, of course, the critical part of the whole thing. It is what I have been yearning for and searching for, so you can be sure I am an eager pupil.

"The first instruction, the most elementary part, consists of having to practice the most difficult physical exercises, all of them concerned with muscle control and breathing. But after some weeks of this, even the eager pupil becomes impatient. I tell the yogi that it is my mental powers I wish to develop, not my physical ones.

"He replies, 'If you will develop control of your body, then the control of your mind will be an automatic thing.' But I want both at once, and I keep asking him, and in the end he says, 'Very well, I will give you some exercises to help you to concentrate the conscious mind.'

" '*Conscious* mind?' I ask. 'Why do you say *conscious* mind?'

" 'Because each man has two minds, the conscious and the subconscious. The subconscious mind is highly concentrated, but the conscious mind, the one everyone uses, is a scattered, unconcentrated thing. It is concerning itself with thousands of different items, the things you are seeing around you and the things you are thinking about. So you must learn to concentrate it in such a way that you can visualize at will *one item,* one item only, and absolutely nothing else. If you work hard at this, you should be able to concentrate your mind, your conscious mind, upon any one object you select for at least three and a half minutes. But that will take about fifteen years.'

" 'Fifteen years!' I cry.

" 'It may take longer,' he says. 'Fifteen years is the usual time.'

" 'But I will be an old man by then!'

" 'Do not despair,' the yogi says. 'The time varies with different people. Some take ten years, a few can take less, and on extremely rare occasions a special person comes along who is able to develop the power in only one or two years. But that is one in a million.'

" 'Who are these special people?' I ask. 'Do they look different from other people?'

" 'They look the same,' he says. 'A special person might be a humble roadsweeper or a factory worker. Or he might be a rajah. There is no way of telling until the training begins.'

" 'Is it really so difficult,' I ask, 'to concentrate the mind upon a single object for three and a half minutes?'

" 'It is almost impossible,' he answers. 'Try it and see. Shut your eyes and think of something. Think of just one object. Visualize it. See it before you. And in a few seconds your mind will start wandering. Other little thoughts will creep in. Other visions will come to you. It is a very difficult thing.'

"Thus spoke the yogi of Hardawar.

"And so my real exercises begin. Each evening, I sit down

and close my eyes and visualize the face of the person I love best, which is my brother. I concentrate upon visualizing his face. But the instant my mind begins to wander, I stop the exercise and rest for some minutes. Then I try again.

"After three years of daily practice, I am able to concentrate absolutely upon my brother's face for one and a half minutes. I am making progress. But an interesting thing happens. In doing these exercises, I lose my sense of smell absolutely. And never to this day does it come back to me.

"Then the necessity for earning my living to buy food forces me to leave Hardawar. I go to Calcutta, where there are greater opportunities, and there I soon begin to make quite good money by giving conjuring performances. But always I continue with the exercises. Every evening, wherever I am, I settle myself down in a quiet corner and practice the concentrating of the mind upon my brother's face. Occasionally, I choose something not so personal, like for example an orange or a pair of spectacles, and that makes it even more difficult.

"One day, I travel from Calcutta to Dacca in East Bengal to give a conjuring show at a college there, and while in Dacca, I happen to be present at a demonstration of walking on fire. There are many people watching. There is a big trench dug at the bottom of a sloping lawn. The spectators are sitting by the hundreds upon the slopes of the lawn looking down upon the trench.

"The trench is about twenty-five feet long. It has been filled with logs and firewood and charcoal, and a lot of paraffin has been poured on it. The paraffin has been lit, and after a while the whole trench has become a smoldering hot furnace. It is so hot that the men who are stoking it are obliged to wear goggles. There is a high wind and the wind fans the charcoal almost to white heat.

"The Indian firewalker then comes forward. He is naked

except for a small loincloth, and his feet are bare. The crowd becomes silent. The firewalker enters the trench and walks the whole length of it, over the white-hot charcoal. He doesn't stop. Nor does he hurry. He simply walks over the white-hot coals and comes out at the other end, and his feet are not even singed. He shows the soles of his feet to the crowd. The crowd stares in amazement.

"Then the firewalker walks the trench once more. This time he goes even slower, and as he does it, I can see on his face a look of pure and absolute concentration. This man, I tell myself, has practiced yoga. He is a yogi.

"After the performance, the firewalker calls out to the crowd, asking if there is anyone brave enough to come down and walk on the fire. There is a hush in the crowd. I feel a sudden surge of excitement in my chest. This is my chance. I must take it. I must have faith and courage. I *must* try it. I have been doing my concentration exercises for over three years now and the time has come to give myself a severe test.

"While I am standing there thinking these thoughts, a volunteer comes forward from the crowd. It is a young Indian man. He announces that he would like to try the firewalk. This decides me, and I also step forward and make my announcement. The crowd gives us both a cheer.

"Now the real firewalker becomes the supervisor. He tells the other man he will go first. He makes him remove his dhoti, otherwise, he says, the hem will catch fire from the heat. And the sandals must be taken off.

"The young Indian does what he is told. But now that he is close to the trench and can feel the terrible heat coming from it, he begins to look frightened. He steps back a few paces, shielding his eyes from the heat with his hands.

" 'You don't have to do it if you don't want to,' the real firewalker says.

"The crowd waits and watches, sensing a drama.

"The young man, though scared out of his wits, wishes to prove how brave he is, and he says, 'Of course I'll do it.'

"With that, he runs toward the trench. He steps into it with one foot, then the other. He gives a fearful scream and leaps out again and falls to the ground. The poor man lies there screaming in pain. The soles of his feet are badly burned and some of the skin has come right away. Two of his friends run forward and carry him off.

" 'Now it is your turn,' says the firewalker. 'Are you ready?'

" 'I am ready,' I say. 'But please be silent while I prepare myself.'

"A great hush has come over the crowd. They have seen one man get badly burned. Is the second one going to be mad enough to do the same thing?

"Someone in the crowd shouts, 'Don't do it! You must be mad!' Others take up the shout, all telling me to give up. I turn and face them and raise my hands for silence. They stop shouting and stare at me. Every eye in that place is upon me now.

"I feel extraordinarily calm.

"I pull my dhoti off over my head. I take off my sandals. I stand there naked except for my underpants. I stand very still and close my eyes. I begin to concentrate my mind. I concentrate on the fire. I see nothing but the white-hot coals and I concentrate on them being not hot but cold. The coals are cold, I tell myself. They cannot burn me. It is impossible for them to burn me because there is no heat in them. I allow half a minute to go by. I know that I must not wait too long because I am only able to concentrate absolutely upon any one thing for a minute and a half.

"I keep concentrating. I concentrate so hard that I go into a sort of trance. I step out onto the coals. I walk fairly fast the whole length of the trench. And behold, I am not burned!

"The crowd goes mad. They yell and cheer. The original firewalker rushes up to me and examines the soles of my feet. He can't believe what he sees. There is not a burn mark on them.

" 'Ayeee!' he cries. 'What is this? Are you a yogi?'

" 'I am on the way, sir,' I answer proudly. 'I am well on the way.'

"After that, I dress and leave quickly, avoiding the crowd.

"Of course I am excited. 'It is coming to me,' I say. 'Now at last the power is beginning to come.' And all the time I am remembering something else. I am remembering a thing that the old yogi of Hardawar said to me. He said, 'Certain holy people have been known to develop so great a concentration that they could see without using their eyes.' I keep remembering that saying and I keep longing for the power to do likewise myself. And after my success with the firewalking, I decide that I will concentrate everything upon this single aim—to see without the eyes."

6

For only the second time so far, Imhrat Khan broke off his story. He took another sip of water, then he leaned back in his chair and closed his eyes.

"I am trying to get everything in the correct order," he said. "I don't want to omit anything."

"You're doing fine," I told him. "Carry on."

"Very well," he said. "So I am still in Calcutta and I have just had success with firewalking. And now I have decided to concentrate all my energy on this one thing, which is to see without the eyes.

"The time has come, therefore, to make a slight change

in the exercises. Each night now I light a candle and I begin
by staring at the flame. A candle flame, you know, has three
separate parts, the yellow at the top, the mauve lower down,
and the black right inside. I place the candle sixteen inches
away from my face. The flame is absolutely level with my
eyes. It must not be above or below. It must be dead level
because then I do not have to make even the tiniest little
adjustment of the eye muscles by looking up or down. I
settle myself comfortably and I begin to stare at the black
part of the flame, right in the center. All this is merely to
concentrate my conscious mind, to empty it of everything
around me. So I stare at the black spot in the flame until
everything around me has disappeared and I can see nothing else. Then slowly I shut my eyes and begin to concentrate as usual upon one single object of my choice, which as
you know is usually my brother's face.

"I do this every night before bed and by 1929, when I am
twenty-four years old, I can concentrate upon an object for
three minutes without any wandering of my mind. So it is
now, at this time, when I am twenty-four, that I begin to
become aware of a slight ability to see an object with my
eyes closed. It is a very slight ability, just a queer little
feeling that when I close my eyes and look at something
hard, with fierce concentration, then I can see the outline of
the object I am looking at.

"Slowly I am beginning to develop my *inner* sense of
sight.

"You ask me what I mean by that. I will explain it to you
exactly as the yogi of Hardawar explained it to me.

"All of us, you see, have two senses of sight, just as we
have two senses of smell and taste and hearing. There is
the outer sense, the highly developed one which we all use,
and there is the *inner* one also. If only we could develop
these inner senses of ours, then we could smell without our

noses, taste without our tongues, hear without our ears and see without our eyes. Do you not understand? Do you not see that our noses and tongues and ears and eyes are only ... how shall I say it? ... are only instruments which assist in conveying the sensation itself to the brain.

"And so it is that I am all the time striving to develop my inner sense of sight. Each night now I perform my usual exercises with the candle flame and my brother's face. After that I rest a little while. I drink a cup of coffee. Then I blindfold myself and I sit in my chair trying to visualize, trying to see, not just to imagine, but actually to *see* without my eyes every object in the room.

"And gradually success begins to come.

"Soon I am working with a pack of cards. I take a card from the top of the pack and hold it before me, back to front, trying to see through it. Then, with a pencil in my other hand, I write down what I think it is. I take another card and do the same again. I go through the whole of the pack like that and when it is over I check what I have written down against the pile of cards beside me. Almost at once I have a sixty to seventy percent success.

"I do other things. I buy maps and complicated navigating charts and pin them up all around my room. I spend hours looking at them blindfold, trying to see them, trying to read the small lettering of the place names and the rivers. Every evening for the next four years, I proceed with this kind of practice.

"By the year 1933—that is only last year—when I am twenty-eight years old, I can read a book. I can cover my eyes completely and I can read a book right through.

"So now at last I have it, this power. For certain I have it now, and at once, because I cannot wait with impatience, I include the blindfold act in my ordinary conjuring performance.

"The audience loves it. They applaud long and loud. But not one single person believes it to be genuine. Everyone thinks it is just another clever trick. And the fact that I am a conjuror makes them think more than ever that I am faking. Conjurors are men who trick you. They trick you with cleverness. And so no one believes me. Even the doctors who blindfold me in the most expert way refuse to believe that anyone can see without his eyes. They forget there may be other ways of sending the image to the brain."

"What other ways?" I asked him.

"Quite honestly, I don't know exactly how it is I can see without my eyes. But what I do know is this: When my eyes are bandaged, I am not using the eyes at all. The seeing is done by another part of my body."

"Which part?" I asked him.

"Any part at all as long as the skin is bare. For example, if you put a sheet of metal in front of me and put a book behind the metal, I cannot read the book. But if you allow me to put my hand around the sheet of metal so that the hand is seeing the book, then I can read it."

"Would you mind if I tested you on that?" I asked.

"Not at all," he answered.

"I don't have a sheet of metal," I said, "but the door will do just as well."

I stood up and went to the bookshelf. I took down the first book that came to hand. It was *Alice's Adventures in Wonderland*. I opened the door and asked my visitor to stand behind it, out of sight. I opened the book at random and propped it on a chair the other side of the door to him. Then I stationed myself in a position where I could see both him and the book.

"Can you read that book?" I asked him.

"No," he answered. "Of course not."

"All right. You may now put your hand around the door, but only the hand."

He slid his hand around the edge of the door until it was within sight of the book. Then I saw the fingers on the hand parting from one another, spreading wide, beginning to quiver slightly, feeling the air like the antennae of an insect. And the hand turned so that the back of it was facing the book.

"Try to read the left page from the top," I said.

There was silence for perhaps ten seconds, then smoothly, without pause, he began to read: " *'Have you guessed the riddle yet?' the Hatter said, turning to Alice again. 'No, I give it up' Alice replied. 'What's the answer?' 'I haven't the slightest idea,' said the Hatter. 'Nor I,' said the March Hare. Alice sighed wearily. 'I think you might do something better with the time,' she said, 'than wasting it in asking riddles that have no answers.'* "

"It's perfect!" I cried. "Now I believe you! You are a miracle!" I was enormously excited.

"Thank you, doctor," he said gravely. "What you say gives me great pleasure."

"One question," I said. "It's about the playing cards. When you held up the reverse side of one of them, did you put your hand around the other side to help you read it?"

"You are very perceptive," he said. "No, I did not. In the case of the cards, I was actually able to *see through* them in some way."

"How do you explain that?" I asked.

"I don't explain it," he said. "Except perhaps that a card is such a flimsy thing, it is so thin, and not solid like metal or thick like a door. That is all the explanation I can give. There are many things in this world, doctor, that we cannot explain."

"Yes," I said. "There certainly are."

"Would you be kind enough to take me home now," he said. "I feel very tired."

I drove him home in my car.

7

That night I didn't go to bed. I was far too worked up to sleep. I had just witnessed a miracle. This man would have doctors all over the world turning somersaults in the air! He could change the whole course of medicine! From a doctor's point of view, he must be the most valuable man alive! We doctors must get hold of him and keep him safe. We must look after him. We mustn't let him go. We must find out exactly how it is that an image can be sent to the brain without using the eyes. And if we do that, then blind people might be able to see and deaf people might be able to hear. Above all, this incredible man must not be ignored and left to wander around India, living in cheap rooms and playing in second-rate theaters.

I got so steamed up thinking about this that after a while I grabbed a notebook and a pen and started writing down with great care everything that Imhrat Khan had told me that evening. I used the notes I had made while he was talking. I wrote for five hours without stopping. And at eight o'clock the next morning, when it was time to go to the hospital, I had finished the most important part, the pages you have just read.

At the hospital that morning, I didn't see Dr. Marshall until we met in the doctors' rest room during our tea break.

I told him as much as I could in the ten minutes we had to spare. "I'm going back to the theater tonight," I said. "I *must* talk to him again. I must persuade him to stay here. We mustn't lose him now."

"I'll come with you," Dr. Marshall said.

"Right," I said. "We'll watch the show first and then we'll take him out to supper."

At a quarter to seven that evening, I drove Dr. Marshall in my car to Acacia Road. I parked the car, and the two of us walked over to the Royal Palace Hall.

"There's something wrong," I said. "Where is everybody?"

There was no crowd outside the hall and the doors were closed. The poster advertising the show was still in place, but I now saw that someone had written across it in large printed letters, using black paint, the words TONIGHT'S PER-FORMANCE CANCELED. There was an old gatekeeper standing by the locked doors.

"What happened?" I asked him.

"Someone died," he said.

"Who?" I asked, knowing already who it was.

"The man who sees without his eyes," the gatekeeper answered.

"How did he die?" I cried. "When? Where?"

"They say he died in his bed," the gatekeeper said. "He went to sleep and never woke up. These things happen."

We walked slowly back to the car. I felt an overwhelming sense of grief and anger. I should never have allowed this precious man to go home last night. I should have kept him. I should have given him my bed and taken care of him. I shouldn't have let him out of my sight. Imhrat Khan was a maker of miracles. He had communicated with mysterious and dangerous forces that are beyond the reach of ordinary people. He had also broken all the rules. He had performed miracles in public. He had taken money for doing so. And, worst of all, he had told some of those secrets to an out-sider—me. Now he was dead.

"So that's that," Dr. Marshall said.

"Yes," I said. "It's all over. Nobody will ever know how he did it."

This is a true and accurate report of everything that took place concerning my two meetings with Imhrat Khan.

(signed)   John F. Cartwright, M.D.

Bombay, December 4, 1934

8

"Well, well, well," said Henry Sugar. "Now *that* is extremely interesting."

He closed the exercise book and sat gazing at the rain splashing against the windows of the library.

"This," Henry Sugar went on, talking aloud to himself, "is a terrific piece of information. It could change my life."

The piece of information Henry was referring to was that Imhrat Khan had trained himself to read the value of a playing card from the reverse side. And Henry the gambler, the rather dishonest gambler, had realized at once that if only *he* could train himself to do the same thing, he could make a fortune.

For a few moments, Henry allowed his mind to dwell upon the marvelous things he would be able to do if he could read cards from the back. He would win every single time at canasta and bridge and poker. And better still, he would be able to go into any casino in the world and clean up at blackjack and all the other high-powered card games they played!

In gambling casinos, as Henry knew very well, nearly everything depended in the end upon the turn of a single card, and if you knew beforehand what the value of that card was, then you were home and dry!

But could he do it? Could he actually train himself to do this thing?

He didn't see why not. That stuff with the candle flame didn't appear to be particularly hard work. And according to the book, that was really all there was to it—just staring into the middle of the flame and trying to concentrate upon the face of the person you loved best.

It would probably take him several years to bring it off, but then who in the world wouldn't be willing to train for a few years in order to beat the casinos every time he went in?

"By golly," he said aloud, "I'll do it! I'm going to do it!"

He sat very still in the armchair in the library, working out a plan of campaign. Above all, he would tell nobody what he was up to. He would steal the little book from the library so that none of his friends might come upon it by chance and learn the secret. He would carry the book with him wherever he went. It would be his bible. He couldn't possibly go out and find a real live yogi to instruct him, so the book would be his yogi instead. It would be his teacher.

Henry stood up and slipped the slim blue exercise book under his jacket. He walked out of the library and went straight upstairs to the bedroom they had given him for the weekend. He got out his suitcase and hid the book underneath his clothes. He then went downstairs again and found his way to the butler's pantry.

"John," he said, addressing the butler, "can you find me a candle? Just an ordinary white candle."

Butlers were trained never to ask for reasons. They simply obeyed orders. "Do you wish a candleholder as well, sir?"

"Yes. A candle and a candleholder."

"Very good, sir. Shall I bring them to your room?"

"No. I'll hang around here till you find them."

The butler soon found a candle and a candleholder. Henry said, "And now could you find me a ruler?" The butler found him a ruler. Henry thanked him and returned to his bedroom.

When he was inside the bedroom, he locked the door. He drew all the curtains so that the place was in twilight. He put the candleholder with the candle in it on the dressing table and pulled up a chair. When he sat down, he noticed with satisfaction that his eyes were exactly level with the wick of the candle. Now, using the ruler, he positioned his face sixteen inches from the candle, which again was what the book had said must be done.

That Indian fellow had visualized the face of the person he loved best, which in his case was a brother. Henry didn't have a brother. He decided instead to visualize his own face. With his cigarette lighter, he lit the wick. A yellow flame appeared and burned steadily.

Henry sat quite still and stared into the candle flame. The book had been quite right. The flame, when you looked into it closely, did have three separate parts. There was the yellow outside. Then there was the mauve inner sheath. And right in the middle was the tiny magic area of absolute blackness. He stared at the tiny black area. He focused his eyes upon it and kept staring at it, and as he did so, an extraordinary thing happened. His mind went absolutely blank, and his brain ceased fidgeting around, and all at once it felt as though he himself, his whole body, was actually encased within the flame, sitting snug and cozy within the little black area of nothingness.

With no trouble at all, Henry allowed the image of his own face to swim into sight before him. He concentrated upon the face and nothing but the face. He blocked out all other thoughts. He succeeded completely in doing this, but only for about fifteen seconds. After that, his mind began to wander and he found himself thinking about gambling casinos and how much money he was going to win. At this point, he looked away from the candle and gave himself a rest.

This was his very first effort. He was thrilled. He had done it. Admittedly he hadn't kept it up for very long. But neither had that Indian fellow on the first attempt.

After a few minutes, he tried again. It went well. He had no stopwatch to time himself with, but he sensed that this was definitely a longer go than the first one.

"It's terrific!" he cried. "I'm going to succeed! I'm going

to do it!" He had never been so excited by anything in his life.

From that day on, no matter where he was or what he was doing, Henry made a point of practicing with the candle every morning and every evening. Often he practiced at midday as well. For the first time in his life he was throwing himself into something with genuine enthusiasm. And the progress he made was remarkable. After six months, he could concentrate absolutely upon his own face for no less than three minutes without a single outside thought entering his mind.

The yogi of Hardawar had told the Indian fellow that a man would have to practice for fifteen years to get that sort of result!

But wait! The yogi had also said something else. He had said (and here Henry eagerly consulted the little blue exercise book for the hundredth time), he had said that on extremely rare occasions a special person comes along who is able to develop the power in only one or two years.

"That's me!" Henry cried. "It must be me! I am the one-in-a-million person who is gifted with the ability to acquire yoga powers at incredible speed! Whoopee and hurray! It won't be long now before I'm breaking the bank in every casino in Europe and America!"

But Henry at this point showed unusual patience and good sense. He didn't rush to get out a pack of cards to see if he could read them from the reverse side. In fact, he kept well away from card games of all kinds. He had given up bridge and canasta and poker as soon as he had started working with the candle. What's more he had given up razzing around to parties and weekends with his rich friends. He had become dedicated to this single aim of acquiring yoga powers, and everything else would have to wait until he had succeeded.

Sometime during the tenth month, Henry became aware,

just as Imhrat Khan had done before him, of a slight ability to see an object with his eyes closed. When he closed his eyes and stared at something hard, with fierce concentration, he could actually see the outline of the object he was looking at.

"It's coming to me!" he cried. "I'm doing it! It's fantastic!"

Now he worked harder than ever at his exercises with the candle, and at the end of the first year he could actually concentrate upon the image of his own face for no less than five and a half minutes!

At this point, he decided the time had come to test himself with the cards. He was in the living room of his London flat when he made this decision, and it was near midnight. He got out a pack of cards and a pencil and paper. He was shaking with excitement. He placed the pack upside down before him and concentrated on the top card.

All he could see at first was the design on the back of the card. It was a very ordinary design of thin red lines, one of the commonest playing-card designs in the world. He now shifted his concentration from the pattern itself to the other side of the card. He concentrated with great intensity upon the invisible underneath of the card, and he allowed no other single thought to creep into his mind. Thirty seconds went by.

Then one minute . . .

Two minutes . . .

Three minutes . . .

Henry didn't move. His concentration was intense and absolute. He was visualizing the reverse side of the playing-card. No other thought of any kind was allowed to enter his head.

During the fourth minute, something began to happen. Slowly, magically, but very clearly, the black symbols became spades and alongside the spades appeared the figure five.

The five of spades!

Henry switched off his concentration. And now, with shaking fingers, he picked up the card and turned it over.

It *was* the five of spades!

"I've done it!" he cried aloud, leaping up from his chair. "I've seen through it! I'm on my way!"

After resting for a while, he tried again, and this time he used a stopwatch to see how long it took him. After three minutes and fifty-eight seconds, he read the card as the king of diamonds. He was right!

The next time he was right again and it took him three minutes and fifty-four seconds. That was four seconds less.

He was sweating with excitement and exhaustion. "That's enough for today," he told himself. He got up and poured himself an enormous drink of whiskey and sat down to rest and to gloat over his success.

His job now, he told himself, was to keep practicing and practicing with the cards until he could see through them instantly. He was convinced it could be done. Already, on the second try, he had knocked four seconds off his time. He would give up working with the candle and concentrate solely upon the cards. He would keep at it day and night.

And that is what he did. But now that he could smell real success in the offing, he became more fanatical than ever. He never left his flat except to buy food and drink. All day and often far into the night, he crouched over the cards with the stopwatch beside him, trying to reduce the time it took him to read from the reverse side.

Within a month, he was down to one and a half minutes.

And at the end of six months of fierce concentrated work, he could do it in twenty seconds. But even that was too long. When you are gambling in a casino and the dealer is waiting for you to say yes or no to the next card, you are not going to be allowed to stare at it for twenty seconds before making up your mind. Three or four seconds would be permissible. But no more.

Henry kept at it. But from now on, it became more and more difficult to improve his speed. To get down from twenty seconds to nineteen took him a week of very hard work. From nineteen to eighteen took him nearly two weeks. And seven more months went by before he could read through a card in ten seconds flat.

His target was four seconds. He knew that unless he could see through a card in a maximum of four seconds, he wouldn't be able to work the casinos successfully. Yet the nearer he got toward the target, the more difficult it became to reach it. It took four weeks to get his time down from ten seconds to nine, and five more weeks to go from nine to eight. But at this stage, hard work no longer bothered him. His powers of concentration had now developed to such a degree that he was able to work for twelve hours at a stretch with no trouble at all. And he knew with absolute certainty that he would get there in the end. He would not stop until he did. Day after day, night after night, he sat crouching over the cards with his stopwatch beside him, fighting with a terrible intensity to knock those last few stubborn seconds off his time.

The last three seconds were the worst of all. To get from seven seconds down to his target of four took him exactly eleven months!

The great moment came on a Saturday evening. A card lay facedown on the table in front of him. He clicked the stopwatch and began to concentrate. At once, he saw a blob of red. The blob swiftly took shape and became a diamond. And then, almost instantaneously, a figure six appeared in the top left-hand corner. He clicked the watch again. He checked the time. It was four seconds! He turned the card over. It was the six of diamonds! He had done it! He had it in four seconds flat!

He tried again with another card. In four seconds he read it as the queen of spades. He went right through the pack, timing himself with every card. Four seconds! Four seconds! Four seconds! It was always the same! He had done it at last! It was all over! He was ready to go!

And how long had it taken him? It had taken him exactly three years and three months of concentrated work.

And now for the casinos!

When should he start?

Why not tonight?

Tonight was Saturday. All the casinos were crowded on Saturday nights. So much the better. There'd be less chance of becoming conspicuous. He went into his bedroom to change into his dinner jacket and black tie. Saturday was a dressy night at the big London casinos.

He would go, he decided, to Lord's House. There are well over one hundred legitimate casinos in London, but none of them is open to the general public. You must become a member before you are allowed to walk in. Henry was a member of no less than ten casinos. Lord's House was his favorite. It was the finest and most exclusive in the country.

9

Lord's House was a magnificent Georgian mansion in the center of London, and for over two hundred years it had been the private residence of a duke. Now it was taken over by the bookmakers, and the superb high-ceilinged rooms where the aristocracy and often royalty used to gather and play a gentle game of whist were today filled with a new kind of people who played a very different sort of game.

Henry drove to Lord's House and pulled up outside the great entrance. He got out of the car but left the engine running. Immediately, an attendant in green uniform came forward to park it for him.

Along the curb on both sides of the street stood perhaps a dozen Rolls Royces. Only the very wealthy belonged to Lord's House.

"Why hello, Mr. Sugar!" said the man behind the desk whose job it was never to forget a face. "We haven't seen you for years!"

"I've been busy," Henry answered.

He went upstairs, up the marvelous wide staircase with its carved mahogany banisters, and entered the cashier's office. There he wrote a check for one thousand pounds. The cashier gave him ten large pink rectangular plaques made of plastic. On each it said £100. Henry slipped them into his pocket and spent a few minutes sauntering through the various gaming rooms to get the feel of things again after such a long absence. There was a big crowd here tonight. Well-fed women stood around the roulette wheel like plump hens around a feeding hopper. Jewels and gold were dripping over their bosoms and from their wrists. Many of them had blue hair. The men were in dinner jackets and there wasn't a tall one among them. Why, Henry wondered, did this particular kind of rich man always have short legs? Their legs all seemed to stop at the knees with no thighs above. Most of them had bellies coming out a long way, and crimson faces and cigars between their lips. Their eyes glittered with greed.

All this Henry noticed. It was the first time in his life that he had looked with distaste upon this type of wealthy gambling-casino person. Up until now, he had always regarded them as companions, as members of the same group and class as himself. Tonight they seemed vulgar.

Could it be, he wondered, that the yoga powers he had acquired over the last three years had altered him just a little bit?

He stood watching the roulette. Upon the long green table people were placing their money, trying to guess which little slot the small white ball would fall into on the next spin of the wheel. Henry looked at the wheel. And suddenly, perhaps more from habit than anything else, he found himself beginning to concentrate upon it. It was not difficult. He had been practicing the art of total concentration for so long that it had become something of a routine. In a fraction of a second, his mind had become completely and absolutely concentrated upon the wheel. Everything else in the room, the noise, the people, the lights, the smell of cigar smoke, all this was wiped out of his mind, and he saw only the round, polished roulette wheel with the small white numbers around the rim. The numbers went from 1 to 36, with a 0 between 1 and 36. Very quickly, all the numbers blurred and disappeared in front of his eyes, all except one, all except the number 18. The 18 was the only number he could see. At first it was slightly fuzzy and out of focus. Then the edges sharpened and the whiteness of it grew brighter, more brilliant, until it began to glow as though there was a bright light behind it. It grew bigger. It seemed to jump toward him. At that point, Henry switched off his concentration. The room swam back into vision.

"Have you all finished?" the croupier was saying.

Henry took a £100 plaque from his pocket and placed it on the square marked 18 on the green table. Although the table was covered all over with other people's bets, his was the only one on 18.

The croupier spun the wheel. The little white ball bounced and skittered around the rim. The people watched. All eyes were on the little ball. The wheel slowed. It came to rest. The ball jiggled a few more times, hesitated, then dropped neatly into slot 18.

"Eighteen!" called the croupier.

The crowd sighed. The croupier's assistant scooped up the piles of losing plaques with a long-handled wooden scooper. But he didn't take Henry's. They paid him thirty-six to one: £3600 for his £100. They gave it to him in three £1000 plaques and six £100s.

Henry began to feel an extraordinary sense of power. He felt he could break this place if he wanted to. He could ruin this fancy high-powered expensive joint in a matter of hours. He could take a million off them and all the stony-faced sleek gentlemen who stood around watching the money rolling in would be scurrying about like panicky rats.

Should he do that?

It was a great temptation.

But it would be the end of everything. He would become famous and would never be allowed into a casino again anywhere in the world. He mustn't do it. He must be very careful not to draw attention to himself.

Henry moved casually out of the roulette room and passed into the room where they were playing blackjack. He stood in the doorway watching the action. There were four tables. They were oddly shaped, these blackjack tables, each one curved like a crescent moon, with the players sitting on high stools around the outside of the half-circle and the dealer standing inside.

The packs of cards (at Lord's House they used four packs shuffled together) lay in an open-ended box known as a *shoe*, and the dealer pulled the cards out of the shoe one by one with his fingers. The reverse side of the first card in the shoe was always visible, but no others.

Blackjack, as the casinos call it, is a very simple game. You and I know it by one of three other names: pontoon,

twenty-one or *vingt-et-un*. The player tries to get his cards
to add up to as near twenty-one as possible, but if he goes
over twenty-one, he's bust and the dealer takes the money.
In nearly every hand, the player is faced with the problem
of whether to draw another card and risk being bust, or
whether to stick with what he's got. But Henry would not
have that problem. In four seconds, he would have "seen
through" the card the dealer was offering him, and he would
know whether to say yes or no. Henry could turn blackjack
into a farce.

In all casinos, they have an awkward rule about blackjack
betting that we do not have at home. At home, we look at
our first card before we make a bet, and if it's a good one
we bet high. The casinos don't allow you to do this. They
insist that everyone at the table makes his bet *before* the
first card of the hand is dealt. What's more, you are not
allowed to increase your bet later on by buying a card.

None of this would disturb Henry either. So long as he
sat on the dealer's immediate left, then he would always
receive the first card in the shoe at the beginning of each
deal. The reverse side of this card would be clearly visible
to him, and he would "read through" it before he made his
bet.

Now, standing quietly just inside the doorway, Henry
waited for a place to become vacant on the dealer's left at
any of the four tables. He had to wait twenty minutes for
this to happen, but he got what he wanted in the end.

He perched himself on the high stool and handed the
dealer one of the £1000 plaques he had won at roulette. "All
in twenty-fives, please," he said.

The dealer was a youngish man with black eyes and gray
skin. He never smiled and he spoke only when necessary.
His hands were exceptionally slim and there was arithmetic
in his fingers. He took Henry's plaque and dropped it into a

slot in the table. Rows of different-colored circular chips lay neatly in a wooden tray in front of him, chips for £25, £10 and £5, maybe a hundred of each. With his thumb and forefinger, the dealer picked up a wedge of £25 chips and placed them in a tall pile on the table. He didn't have to count them. He knew there were exactly twenty chips in the pile. Those nimble fingers could pick up with absolute accuracy any number of chips from one to twenty and never be wrong. The dealer picked up a second lot of twenty chips, making forty in all. He slid them over the table to Henry.

Henry stacked the chips in front of him, and as he did so, he glanced at the top card in the shoe. He switched on his concentration and in four seconds he read it as a ten. He pushed out eight of his chips, £200. This was the maximum stake allowed for blackjack at Lord's House.

He was dealt the ten, and for his second card he got a nine, nineteen altogether.

Everyone sticks on nineteen. You sit tight and hope the dealer won't get twenty or twenty-one.

So when the dealer came around again to Henry, he said, "Nineteen," and passed on to the next player.

"Wait," Henry said.

The dealer paused and came back to Henry. He raised his brows and looked at him with those cool black eyes. "You wish to draw to nineteen?" he asked somewhat sarcastically. He spoke with an Italian accent, and there was scorn as well as sarcasm in his voice. There were only two cards in the pack that would not bust a nineteen, the ace (counting as a one) and the two. Only an idiot would risk drawing to nineteen, especially with £200 on the table.

The next card to be dealt lay clearly visible in the front of the shoe. At least, the reverse side of it was clearly visible. The dealer hadn't yet touched it.

"Yes," Henry said, "I think I'll have another card."

The dealer shrugged and flipped the card out of the shoe. The two of clubs landed neatly in front of Henry, alongside the ten and the nine.

"Thank you," Henry said. "That will do nicely."

"Twenty-one," the dealer said. His black eyes glanced up again into Henry's face, and they rested there, silent, watchful, puzzled. Henry had unbalanced him. He had never in his life seen anyone draw to a nineteen. This fellow had drawn to nineteen with a calmness and a certainty that was quite staggering. And he had won.

Henry caught the look in the dealer's eyes, and he realized at once that he had made a silly mistake. He had been too clever. He had drawn attention to himself. He must never do that again. He must be very careful in the future how he used his powers. He must even make himself lose occasionally, and every now and again he must do something a bit stupid.

The game went on. Henry's advantage was so enormous, he had difficulty keeping his winnings down to a reasonable sum. Every now and again, he would ask for a third card when he already knew it was going to bust him. And once, when he saw that his first card was going to be an ace, he put out his smallest stake, then made a great show of cursing himself aloud for not having made a bigger bet in the first place.

In an hour, he had won exactly £3000, and there he stopped. He pocketed his chips and made his way back to the cashier's office to turn them in for real money.

He had made £3000 from blackjack and £3600 from roulette, £6600 in all. It could just as easily have been £660,000. As a matter of fact, he told himself, he was now almost certainly able to make money faster than any other man in the entire world.

The cashier received Henry's pile of chips and plaques

without twitching a muscle. He wore steel spectacles, and the pale eyes behind the spectacles were not interested in Henry. They looked only at the chips on the counter. This man also had arithmetic in his fingers. But he had more than that. He had arithmetic, trigonometry and calculus and algebra and Euclidean geometry in every nerve of his body. He was a human calculating machine with a hundred thousand electric wires in his brain. It took him five seconds to count Henry's one hundred and twenty chips.

"Would you like a cheque for this, Mr. Sugar?" he asked. The cashier, like the man at the desk downstairs, knew every member by name.

"No, thank you," Henry said, "I'll take it in cash."

"As you wish," said the voice behind the spectacles, and he turned away and went to a safe at the back of the office that must have contained millions.

By Lord's House standards, Henry's win was fairly small potatoes. The Arab oil boys were in London now, and they liked to gamble. So did the shady diplomats from the Far East and the Japanese businessmen and the British tax-dodging real-estate operators. Staggering sums of money were being won and lost, mostly lost, in the large London casinos every day.

The cashier returned with Henry's money and dropped the bundle of notes on the counter. Although there was enough there to buy a small house or a large automobile, the chief cashier at Lord's House was not impressed. He might just as well have been passing Henry a pack of chewing gum for all the notice he took of the money he was dishing out.

"You wait, my friend," Henry thought to himself as he pocketed the money. "You just wait." He walked away.

"Your car, sir?" said the man at the door in the green uniform.

"Not yet," Henry told him. "I think I'll take a bit of fresh air first."

He strolled away down the street. It was nearly midnight. The evening was cool and pleasant. The great city was still wide awake. Henry could feel the bulge in the inside pocket of his jacket where the big wad of money was lying. He touched the bulge with one hand. He patted it gently. It was a lot of money for an hour's work.

And what of the future?

What was the next move going to be?

He could make a million in a month.

He could make more if he wanted to.

There was no limit to what he could make.

Walking through the streets of London in the cool of the evening, Henry began to think about the next move.

Now, had this been a made-up story instead of a true one, it would have been necessary to invent some sort of a surprising and exciting end for it. It would not be difficult to do that. Something dramatic and unusual. So before telling you what really *did* happen to Henry in real life, let us pause here for a moment to see what a competent fiction writer would have done to wrap up this story. His notes would read something like this:

1. Henry must die. Like Imhrat Khan before him, he had violated the code of the yogi and had used his powers for personal gain.

2. It will be best if he dies in some unusual and interesting manner that will surprise the reader.

3. For example, he could go home to his flat and start counting his money and gloating over it. While doing this, he might suddenly begin to

feel unwell. He has a pain in his chest.

4. He becomes frightened. He decides to go to bed immediately and rest. He takes off his clothes. He walks naked to the closet to get his pajamas. He passes the full-length mirror that stands against the wall. He stops. He stares at the reflection of his naked self in the mirror. Automatically, from force of habit he begins to concentrate. And then . . .

5. All at once, he is "seeing through" his own skin. He "sees through" it in the same way that he "saw through" those playing cards a while back. It is like an X-ray picture, only far better. An X-ray can see only the bones and the very dense areas. Henry can see everything. He sees his arteries and veins with the blood pumping through him. He can see his liver, his kidneys, his intestines and he can see his heart beating.

6. He looks at the place in his chest where the pain is coming from . . . and he sees . . . or thinks he sees . . . a small dark lump inside the big vein leading into the heart on the right hand side. What could a small dark lump be doing inside the vein? It must be a blockage of some kind. It must be a clot. A blood clot!

7. At first, the clot seems to be stationary. Then it moves. The movement is very slight, no more than a millimeter or two. The blood inside the vein is pumping up behind the clot and pushing past it and the little clot moves again. It jerks forward about half an inch. This time, up the vein, toward the heart. Henry watches in terror. He knows, as almost everyone else in the world knows, that a blood clot that has broken

free and is traveling in a vein will ultimately
reach the heart. When it reaches the heart, you
often die. . . .

That wouldn't be such a bad ending for a work of fiction,
but this story is not fiction. It is true. The only untrue
things about it are Henry's name and the name of the gambling casino. Henry's name was not Henry Sugar. His name
has to be protected. It still must be protected. And for obvious reasons, one cannot call the casino by its real name.
Apart from that, it is a true story.

And because it is a true story, it must have the true
ending. The true one may not be quite so dramatic or spooky
as a made-up one could be, but it is nonetheless interesting.
Here is what actually happened.

10

After walking the London streets for about an hour, Henry
returned to Lord's House and collected his car. Then he
drove back to his flat. He was a puzzled man. He couldn't
understand why he felt so little excitement about his tremendous success. If this sort of thing had happened to him
three years ago, before he'd started the yoga business, he'd
have gone crazy with excitement. He'd have been dancing
in the streets and rushing off to the nearest nightclub to
celebrate with champagne.

The funny thing was that he didn't really feel excited
at all. He felt melancholy. It had somehow all been too easy.
Every time he'd made a bet, he'd been certain of winning.
There was no thrill, no suspense, no danger of losing. He
knew, of course, that from now on he could travel around
the world and make millions. But was it going to be any
fun doing it?

It was slowly beginning to dawn upon Henry that nothing

is any fun if you can get as much of it as you want. Especially money.

Another thing. Was it not possible that the process he had gone through in order to acquire yoga powers had completely changed his outlook on life?

Certainly it was possible.

Henry drove home and went straight to bed.

The next morning he woke up late. But he didn't feel any more cheerful now than he had the night before. And when he got out of bed and saw the enormous bundle of money still lying on his dressing table, he felt a sudden and very acute revulsion toward it. He didn't want it. For the life of him, he couldn't explain why this was so, but the fact remained that he simply did not want any part of it.

He picked up the bundle. It was all in twenty-pound notes, three hundred and thirty of them to be exact. He walked onto the balcony of his flat, and there he stood in his dark-red silk pajamas looking down at the street below him.

Henry's flat was in Curzon Street, which is right in the middle of London's most fashionable and expensive district, known as Mayfair. One end of Curzon Street runs into Berkeley Square, the other into Park Lane. Henry lived three floors above street level, and outside his bedroom there was a small balcony with iron railings that overhung the street.

The month was June, the morning was full of sunshine, and the time was about eleven o'clock. Although it was a Sunday, there were quite a few people strolling about on the sidewalks.

Henry peeled off a single twenty-pound note from his wad and dropped it over the balcony. A breeze took hold of it and blew it sideways in the direction of Park Lane. Henry stood watching it. It fluttered and twisted in the air and eventually came to rest on the opposite side of the street, directly in front of an old man. The old man was wearing a long, brown, shabby overcoat and a floppy hat, and he was walking slowly, all by himself. He caught sight of the note as it fluttered past his face, and he stopped and picked it up. He held it with both hands and stared at it. He turned it over. He peered closer. Then he raised his head and looked up.

"Hey there!" Henry shouted, cupping a hand to his mouth. "That's for you! It's a present!"

The old man stood quite still, holding the note in front of him and gazing up at the figure on the balcony above.

"Put it in your pocket!" Henry shouted. "Take it home!" His voice carried far along the street, and many people stopped and looked up.

Henry peeled off another note and threw it down. The watchers below him didn't move. They simply watched. They had no idea what was going on. A man was up there on the balcony and he had shouted something, and now he had just thrown down what looked like a piece of paper. Everyone followed the piece of paper as it went fluttering down, and this one came near to a young couple who were standing arm in arm on the sidewalk across the street. The man unlinked his arm and tried to catch the paper as it went past him. He missed it but picked it up from the ground. He examined it closely. The watchers on both sides of the street all had their eyes on the young man now. To many of them, the paper had looked very much like a banknote of some kind, and they were waiting to find out.

"It's twenty pounds!" the man yelled, jumping up and down. "It's a twenty-pound note!"

"Keep it!" Henry shouted at him. "It's yours!"

"You mean it?" the man called back, holding the note out at arm's length. "Can I really keep it?"

Suddenly there was a rustle of excitement along both

sides of the street, and everyone started moving at once. They ran out into the middle of the road and clustered underneath the balcony. They lifted their arms above their heads and started calling out, "Me! How about one for me! Drop us another one, guv'ner! Send down a few more!"

Henry peeled off another five or six notes and threw them down.

There were screams and yells as the pieces of paper fanned out in the wind and floated downward, and there was a good old-fashioned scrimmage in the streets as they reached the hands of the crowd. But it was all very good-natured. People were laughing. They thought it a fantastic joke. Here was a man standing three floors up, in his pajamas, slinging these enormously valuable notes into the air. Quite a few of those present had never even seen a twenty-pound note in their lives before this moment.

But now something else was beginning to happen.

The speed with which news will spread along the streets of a city is phenomenal. The news of what Henry was doing flashed like lightning up and down the length of Curzon Street and into the smaller and larger streets beyond. From all sides, people came running. Within a few minutes, about a thousand men and women and children were blocking the road underneath Henry's balcony. Drivers, who couldn't get through, got out of their cars and joined the crowd. And all of a sudden, there was chaos in Curzon Street.

At this point, Henry simply raised his arm and swung it out and flung the entire bundle of notes into the air. More than six thousand pounds went fluttering down toward the screaming crowd below.

The scramble that followed was really something to see. People were jumping up to catch the notes before they reached the ground, and everyone was pushing and jostling and yelling and falling over, and soon the whole place was a mass of tangled, yelling, fighting human beings.

Above the noise and behind him in his own flat, Henry suddenly heard his front-door bell ringing long and loud. He went in from the balcony and opened the door. A large policeman with a black moustache stood outside with his hands on his hips. "You!" he bellowed angrily. "You're the one! What the devil d'you think you're doing?"

"Good morning, officer," Henry said. "I'm sorry about the crowd. I didn't think it would turn out like that. I was just giving away some money."

"You are causing a nuisance!" the policeman bellowed. "You are creating an obstruction! You are inciting a riot and you are blocking the entire street!"

"I said I was sorry," Henry answered. "I won't do it again, I promise. They'll soon go away."

The policeman took one hand off his hip and from the inside of his palm he produced a twenty-pound note.

"Ah-ha!" Henry cried. "You got one yourself! I'm so glad! I'm so happy for you!"

"Now you just stop that larking about!" the policeman said, "because I have a few serious questions to ask you about these here twenty-pound notes." He took a notebook from his breast pocket. "In the first place," he went on, "where exactly did you get them from?"

"I won them," Henry said. "I had a lucky night." He went on to give the name of the club where he had won the money, and the policeman wrote it down in his little book. "Check it up," Henry added. "They'll tell you it's true."

The policeman lowered the notebook and looked Henry in the eye. "As a matter of fact," he said, "I believe your story. I think you're telling the truth. But that doesn't excuse what you did one little bit."

"I didn't do anything wrong," Henry said.

"You're a blithering young idiot!" the policeman shouted, beginning to work himself up all over again. "You're an ass and an imbecile! If you've been lucky enough to win yourself a tremendous big sum of money like that and you want to give it away, you don't throw it out the window!"

"Why not?" Henry asked, grinning. "It's as good a way of getting rid of it as any."

"It's a damned stupid silly way of getting rid of it!" the policeman cried. "Why didn't you give it where it would do some good? To a hospital, for instance? Or an orphange? There's orphanages all over the country that hardly have enough money to buy the kids a present even for Christmas! And then along comes a little twit like you who's never even known what it's like to be hard up and you throw the stuff out into the street! It makes me mad, it really does!"

"An orphanage?" Henry said.

"Yes, an *orphanage!*" the policeman cried. "I was brought up in one so I ought to know what it's like!" With that, the policeman turned away and went quickly down the stairs toward the street.

Henry didn't move. The policeman's words, and more especially the genuine fury with which they had been spoken, smacked our hero right between the eyes.

"An orphanage?" he cried aloud. "That's quite a thought. But why only one orphanage? Why not lots of them?" And now, very quickly, there began to come to him the great and marvelous idea that was to change everything.

Henry shut the front door and went back into his flat. All at once, he felt a powerful excitement stirring in his belly. He started pacing up and down, ticking off the points that would make his marvelous idea possible.

"One," he said, "I can get hold of a very large sum of money each day of my life.

"Two. I must not go to the same casino more than once every twelve months.

"Three. I must not win too much from any one casino or somebody will get suspicious. I suggest I keep it down to twenty thousand pounds a night.

"Four. Twenty thousand pounds a night for three hundred and sixty-five days in the year comes to how much?"

Henry took a pencil and paper and worked this one out.

"It comes to seven million, three hundred thousand pounds," he said aloud.

"Very well. Point number five. I shall have to keep moving. No more than two or three nights at a stretch in any one city or the word will get around. Go from London to Monte Carlo. Then to Cannes. To Biarritz. To Deauville. To Las Vegas. To Mexico City. To Buenos Aires. To Nassau. And so on.

"Six. With the money I make, I will set up an absolutely first-class orphanage in every country I visit. I will become a Robin Hood. I will take money from the bookmakers and the gambling proprietors and give it to the children. Does that sound corny and sentimental? As a dream, it does. But as a reality, if I can really make it work, it won't be corny at all, or sentimental. It would be rather tremendous.

"Seven. I will need somebody to help me, a man who will sit at home and take care of all that money and buy the houses and organize the whole thing. A money man. Someone I can trust. What about John Winston?"

11

John Winston was Henry's accountant. He handled his income-tax affairs, his investments and all other problems that had to do with money. Henry had known him for eighteen years, and a friendship had developed between the two men. Remember though, that up until now, John Winston had known Henry only as the wealthy idle playboy who had never done a day's work in his life.

"You must be mad," John Winston said when Henry told him his plan. "Nobody has ever devised a system for beating the casinos."

From his pocket, Henry produced a brand-new unopened pack of cards. "Come on," he said. "We'll play a little blackjack. You're the dealer. And don't tell me those cards are marked. It's a new pack."

Solemnly, for nearly an hour, sitting in Winston's office whose windows looked out over Berkeley Square, the two men played blackjack. They used matchsticks as counters, each match being worth twenty-five pounds. After fifty minutes, Henry was no less than thirty-four thousand pounds ahead!

John Winston couldn't believe it. "How do you do it?" he said.

"Put the pack on the table," Henry said. "Face down."

Winston obeyed.

Henry concentrated on the top card for four seconds. "That's a knave of hearts," he said. It was.

"The next one is . . . a three of hearts." It was. He went right through the entire pack, naming every card.

"Go on," John Winston said. "Tell me how you do it." This usually calm and mathematical man was leaning forward over his desk, staring at Henry with eyes as big and bright as two stars. "You do realize you are doing something completely impossible?" he said.

"It's not impossible," Henry said. "It is only very difficult. I am the one man in the world who can do it."

The telephone rang on John Winston's desk. He lifted the receiver and said to his secretary, "No more calls please, Susan, until I tell you. Not even my wife." He looked up, waiting for Henry to go on.

Henry then proceeded to explain to John Winston exactly how he had acquired the power. He told him how he had found the notebook and about Imhrat Khan and then he described how he had been working nonstop for the past three years, training his mind to concentrate.

When he had finished, John Winston said, "Have you tried walking on fire?"

"No," Henry said, "and I'm not going to."

"What makes you think you'll be able to do this thing with the cards in a casino?"

Henry then told him about his visit to Lord's House the night before.

"Six thousand, six hundred pounds!" John Winston cried. "Did you honestly win that much in real money?"

"Listen," Henry said. "I just won thirty-four thousand from you in less than an hour!"

"So you did."

"Six thousand was the very least I could win," Henry said. "It was a terrific effort not to win more."

"You will be the richest man on earth."

"I don't want to be the richest man on earth," Henry said. "Not anymore." He then told him about his plan for orphanages.

When he had finished, he said, "Will you join me, John? Will you be my money man, my banker, my administrator and everything else? There will be millions coming in every year."

John Winston, a cautious and prudent accountant, would not agree to anything at all on the spur of the moment. "I want to see you in action first," he said.

So that night, they went together to the Ritz Club on Curzon Street. "Can't go to Lord's House again now for some time," Henry said.

On the first spin of the roulette wheel, Henry staked £100 on number 27. It came up. The second time he put it on number 4; that came up too. A total of £7200 profit.

An Arab standing next to Henry said, "I have just lost fifty-five thousand pounds. How do you do it?"

"Luck," Henry said. "Just luck."

They moved into the blackjack room and there, in half an hour, Henry won a further £10,000. Then he stopped.

Outside in the street, John Winston said, "I believe you now. I'll come with you."

"We start tomorrow," Henry said.

"Do you really intend to do this every single night?"

"Yes," Henry said. "I shall move very fast from place to place, from country to country. And every day, I shall send the profits back to you through the banks."

"Do you realize how much it will add up to in a year?"

"Millions," Henry said cheerfully. "About seven million a year."

"In that case, I can't operate out of this country," John Winston said. "The taxman will have it all."

"Go anywhere you like," Henry said. "It makes no difference to me. I trust you completely."

"I shall go to Switzerland," John Winston said. "But not tomorrow. I can't just pull up and fly away. I'm not an unattached bachelor like you with no responsibilities. I must talk to my wife and children. I must give notice to my partners in the firm. I must sell my house. I must find another house in Switzerland. I must take the kids out of school. My dear man, these things take time!"

Henry drew from his pocket the £17,500 he had just won and handed them to the other man. "Here's some petty cash to tide you over until you get settled," he said. "But do hurry up. I want to get cracking."

Within a week, John Winston was in Lausanne, with an office high up on the lovely hillside above Lake Geneva. His family would follow him as soon as possible.

And Henry went to work in the casinos.

12

One year later, he had sent a little over eight million pounds to John Winston in Lausanne. The money was sent five days a week to a Swiss company called ORPHANAGES S.A. Nobody except John Winston and Henry knew where the money came from or what was going to happen to it. As for the Swiss authorities, they never want to know where money comes from. Henry sent the money through the banks. The Monday remittance was always the biggest because it included Henry's take for Friday, Saturday and Sunday, when the banks were closed. He moved with astonishing speed, and often the only clue that John Winston had to his whereabouts was the address of the bank that had sent the money on a particular day. One day it would come perhaps from a bank in Manila. The next day from Bangkok. It came from Las Vegas, from Curaçao, from Freeport, from Grand Cayman, from San Juan, from Nassau, from London, from Biarritz. It came from anywhere and everywhere as long as there was a big casino in the city.

13

For seven years, all went well. Nearly fifty million pounds had arrived in Lausanne and had been safely banked away. Already, John Winston had got three orphanages established, one in France, one in England, and one in the United States. Five more were on the way.

Then came a bit of trouble. There is a grapevine among casino owners, and although Henry was always extraordinarily careful not to take too much from any one place on any one night, the news was bound to spread in the end.

They got wise to him one night in Las Vegas when Henry rather imprudently took one hundred thousand dollars from each of three separate casinos that all happened to be owned by the same mob.

What happened was this. The morning after, when Henry was in his hotel room packing to leave for the airport, there was a knock on his door. A bellhop came in and whispered to Henry that two men were waiting for him in the lobby. Other men, the bellhop said, were guarding the rear exit. These were very hard men, the bellhop said, and he did not give much for Henry's chances of survival if he were to go downstairs at this moment.

"Why do you come and tell me?" Henry asked him. "Why are you on my side?"

"I'm not on anyone's side," the bellhop said. "But we all know you won a lot of money last night and I figured you might give me a nice present for tipping you off."

"Thanks," Henry said. "But how do I get away? I'll give you a thousand dollars if you can get me out of here."

"That's easy," the bellhop said. "Take your own clothes off and put on my uniform. Then walk out through the lobby with your suitcase. But tie me up before you leave. I've gotta by lying here on the floor tied up hand and foot so they won't think I helped you. I'll say you had a gun and I couldn't do nothing."

"Where's the cord to tie you up with?" Henry asked.

"Right here in my pocket," the bellhop said, grinning.

Henry put on the bellhop's gold and green uniform, which wasn't too bad a fit. Then he tied the man up good and proper with the cord and stuffed a handkerchief in his mouth. Finally, he pushed ten one-hundred-dollar bills under the carpet for the bellhop to collect later.

Down in the lobby, two short, thick, black-haired thugs were watching the people as they came out of the elevators. But they hardly glanced at the man in the green and gold bellhop's uniform who came out carrying a suitcase and who walked smartly across the lobby and out through the revolving doors that led to the street.

At the airport, Henry changed his flight and took the next plane to Los Angeles. Things were not going to be quite so easy from now on, he told himself. But that bellhop had given him an idea.

In Los Angeles, and in nearby Hollywood and Beverly Hills, where all the film people live, Henry sought out the very best makeup man in the business. This was Max Engelman. Henry called on him. He liked him immediately.

"How much do you earn?" Henry asked him.

"Oh, about forty thousand dollars a year," Max told him.

"I'll give you a hundred thousand," Henry said, "if you will come with me and be my makeup artist."

"What's the big idea?" Max asked him.

"I'll tell you," Henry said. And he did.

Max was only the second person Henry had told. John Winston was the first. And when Henry showed Max how he could read the cards, Max was flabbergasted.

"Great heavens, man!" he cried. "You could make a fortune!"

"I already have," Henry told him. "I've made ten fortunes. But I want to make ten more." He told Max about the orphanages. With John Winston's help, he had already set up seven of them in seven different countries.

Max was a small dark-skinned man who had escaped from Vienna when the Nazis went in. He had never married. He had no ties. He became wildly enthusiastic. "It's crazy!" he cried. "It's the craziest thing I've heard in my life! I'll join you, man! Let's go!"

From then on, Max Engelman traveled everywhere with Henry and carried with him in a trunk such an assortment of wigs, false beards, sideburns, moustaches and makeup materials as you have never seen. He could turn his master into any one of thirty of forty unrecognizable people, and the casino managers, who were all watching for Henry now, never once saw him again as Mr. Henry Sugar. As a matter of fact, only a year after the Las Vegas episode, Henry and

Max actually went back to that dangerous city, and on a warm starry night Henry took a cool eighty thousand dollars from the first of the big casinos he had visited before. He went disguised as an elderly Brazilian diplomat, and they never knew what hit them.

Now that Henry no longer appeared as himself in the casinos, there were, of course, a number of other details that had to be taken care of, such as false identity cards and passports. In Monte Carlo, for example, a visitor must always show his passport before being allowed to enter the casino. Henry visited Monte Carlo eleven more times with Max's assistance, every time with a different passport and in a different disguise.

Max adored the work. He loved creating new characters for Henry. "I have an entirely fresh one for you today!" he would announce. "Just wait till you see it! Today you will be an Arab sheik from Kuwait!"

"Do we have an Arab passport?" Henry would ask. "And Arab papers?"

"We have everything," Max would answer. "John Winston has sent me a lovely passport in the name of His Royal Highness Sheik Abu Bin Bey!"

And so it went on. Over the years, Max and Henry became as brothers. They were crusading brothers, two men who moved swiftly through the skies, milking the casinos of the world and sending the money straight back to John Winston in Switzerland, where the company known as ORPHANAGES S.A. grew richer and richer.

14

Henry died last year, at the age of sixty-three, his work completed. He had been at it for just on twenty years.

His personal reference book listed three hundred and seventy-one major casinos in twenty-one different countries or islands. He had visited them all many times, and he had never lost.

According to John Winston's accounts, he had made altogether £144 million.

He left twenty-one well-established, well-run orphanages scattered about the world, one in each country he visited. All these were administered and financed from Lausanne by John and his staff.

But how do I, who am neither Max Engelman nor John Winston, happen to know all this? And how did I come to write the story in the first place?

I will tell you.

Soon after Henry's death, John Winston telephoned me from Switzerland. He introduced himself simply as the head of a company calling itself ORPHANAGES S.A., and asked me if I would come out to Lausanne to see him with a view to writing a brief history of the organization. I don't know how he got hold of my name. He probably had a list of writers and stuck a pin into it. He would pay me well, he said. And he added, "A remarkable man has died recently. His name was Henry Sugar. I think people ought to know a bit about what he has done."

In my ignorance, I asked whether the story was really interesting enough to merit being put on paper.

"All right," said the man who now controlled £144 million. "Forget it, I'll ask someone else. There are plenty of writers around."

That needled me. "No," I said. "Wait. Could you at least tell me who this Henry Sugar was and what he did? I've never even heard of him."

In five minutes on the phone, John Winston told me something about Henry Sugar's secret career. It was secret no longer. Henry was dead and would never gamble again. I listened, enthralled.

"I'll be on the next plane," I said.

"Thank you," John Winston said. "I would appreciate that."

In Lausanne, I met John Winston, now over seventy, and also Max Engleman, who was about the same age. They were both still shattered by Henry's death, Max even more so than John Winston, for Max had been beside him constantly for over thirteen years. "I loved him," Max said, a shadow falling over his face. "He was a great man. He never thought about himself. He never kept a penny of the money he won, except what he needed to travel and to eat. Listen, once we were in Biarritz and he had just been to the bank and given them half a million francs to send home to John. It was lunchtime. We went to a place and had a simple lunch, an omelete and a bottle of wine, and when the bill came, Henry hadn't got anything to pay it with. I hadn't either. He was a lovely man."

John Winston told me everything he knew. He showed me the original dark-blue notebook written by Dr. John Cartwright in Bombay in 1934 about Imhrat Khan, and I copied it out word for word.

"Henry always carried it with him," John Winston said. "In the end, he knew the whole thing by heart."

He showed me the account books of ORPHANAGES S.A. with Henry's winnings recorded in them day by day over twenty years, and a truly staggering sight they were.

When he had finished, I said to him, "There's a big gap in this story, Mr. Winston. You've told me almost nothing about Henry's travels and about his adventures in the casinos of the world."

"That's Max's story," John Winston said. "Max knows all about that because he was with him. But he says he wants to have a shot at writing it himself. He's already started."

"Then why not let Max write the whole thing?" I asked.

"He doesn't want to," John Winston said. "He only wants to write about Henry and Max. It should be a fantastic story if he ever gets it finished. But he is old now, like me, and I doubt he will manage it."

"One last question," I said. "You keep calling him Henry Sugar. And yet you tell me that wasn't his name. Don't you want me to say who he really was when I do the story?"

"No," John Winston said. "Max and I promised never to reveal it. Oh, it'll probably leak out sooner or later. After all, he was from a fairly well known English family. But I'd appreciate it if you don't try to find out. Just call him plain Mr. Henry Sugar."

And that is what I have done.

Lucky Break–

How I Became a Writer

A fiction writer is a person who invents stories.

But how does one start out on a job like this? How does one become a full-time professional fiction writer?

Charles Dickens found it easy. At the age of twenty-four, he simply sat down and wrote *Pickwick Papers*, which became an immediate best seller. But Dickens was a genius, and geniuses are different from the rest of us.

In this century (it was not always so in the last one), just about every single writer who has finally become successful in the world of fiction has started out in some other job—a schoolteacher, perhaps, or a doctor or a journalist or a lawyer. (*Alice's Adventure in Wonderland* was written by a mathematician, and the *The Wind in the Willows* by a civil servant.) The first attempts at writing have therefore always had to be done in spare time, usually at night.

The reason for this is obvious. When you are grown-up, it is necessary to earn a living. To earn a living, you must get a job. You must, if possible, get a job that guarantees you so much money a week. But however much you may want to take up fiction writing as a career, it would be pointless to go along to a publisher and say, "I want a job as a fiction writer." If you did that, he would tell you to buzz off and write the book first. And even if you brought a finished book to him and he liked it well enough to publish it, he still wouldn't give you a job. He would give you an advance of perhaps one or two thousand dollars, which he would get back again later by deducting it from your royalties. (A royalty, by the way, is the money that a writer gets from the publisher for each copy of his book that is sold. The average royalty a writer gets is 10 percent of the price of the book itself in the bookshop. Thus, for a book selling at seven dollars, the writer would get seventy cents.)

It is very common for a hopeful fiction writer to spend two years of his spare time writing a book which no publisher will publish. For that he gets nothing at all except a sense of frustration.

If he is fortunate enough to have a book accepted by a publisher, the odds are that as a first novel it will sell only about three thousand copies. That will earn him about twenty-one hundred dollars. Most novels take at least one year to write, and twenty-one hundred dollars a year is not enough to live on these days. So you can see why a budding fiction writer invariably has to start out in another job first of all. If he doesn't, he will almost certainly starve.

Here are some of the qualities you should possess or should try to acquire if you wish to become a fiction writer:

1. You should have a lively imagination.
2. You should be able to write well. By that I mean you should be able to make a scene come alive in the reader's mind. Not everybody has this ability. It is a gift, and you either have it or you don't.
3. You must have stamina. In other words, you must be able to stick to what you are doing and never give up, for hour after hour, day after day, week after week, and month after month.
4. You must be a perfectionist. That means you must never be satisfied with what you have written until you have rewritten it again and again, making it as good as you possibly can.
5. You must have strong self-discipline. You are

working alone. No one is employing you. No one is around to fire you if you don't turn up for work, or to tick you off if you start slacking.

6. It helps a lot if you have a keen sense of humor. This is not essential when writing for grown-ups, but for children, it's vital.

7. You must have a degree of humility. The writer who thinks that his work is marvelous is heading for trouble.

Let me try to tell you how I myself slid in through the back door and found myself in the world of fiction.

At the age of eight, in 1924, I was sent away to boarding school in a town called Weston-Super-Mare, on the southwest coast of England. Those were days of horror, of fierce discipline, of no talking in the dormitories, no running in the corridors, no untidiness of any sort, no this or that or the other, just rules, rules and still more rules that had to be obeyed. And the fear of the dreaded cane hung over us like the fear of death all the time.

"The headmaster wants to see you in his study." Words of doom. They sent shivers over the skin of your stomach. But off you went, aged perhaps nine years old, down the long bleak corridors and through an archway that took you into the headmaster's private area where only horrible things happened and the smell of pipe tobacco hung in the air like incense. You stood outside the awful black door, not daring even to knock. You took deep breaths. If only your mother had been here, you told yourself, she would not let this happen. She wasn't here. You were alone. You lifted a hand and knocked softly, once.

"Come in! Ah yes, it's Dahl. Well Dahl, it's been reported to me that you were talking during prep last night."

"Please sir, I broke my nib and I was only asking

Jenkins if he had another one to lend me."

"I will not tolerate talking in prep. You know that very well."

Already this giant of a man was crossing to the tall corner cupboard and reaching up to the top of it where he kept his canes.

"Boys who break rules have to be punished."

"Sir . . . I . . . I had a bust nib . . . I . . ."

"That is no excuse. I am going to teach you that it does not pay to talk during prep."

He took down a cane that was about three feet long with a little curved handle at one end. It was thin and white and very whippy. "Bend over and touch your toes. Over there by the window."

"But, sir . . ."

"Don't argue with me, boy. Do as you're told."

I bent over. Then I waited. He always kept you waiting for about ten seconds, and that was when your knees began to shake.

"Bend lower, boy! Touch your toes!"

I stared at the toecaps of my black shoes and I told myself that any moment now this man was going to bash the cane into me so hard that the whole of my bottom would change color. The welts were always very long, stretching right across both buttocks, blue-black with brilliant scarlet edges, and when you ran your fingers over them ever so gently afterward, you could feel the corrugations.

Swish! . . . Crack!

Then came the pain. It was unbelievable, unbearable, excruciating. It was as though someone had laid a white-hot poker across your backside and pressed hard.

The second stroke would be coming soon and it was as much as you could do to stop putting your hands in the way to ward it off. It was the instinctive reaction. But if you did that, it would break your fingers.

Swish! . . . Crack!

The second one landed right alongside the first and the white-hot poker was pressing deeper and deeper into the skin.

Swish! . . . Crack!

The third stroke was where the pain always reached its peak. It could go no further. There was no way it could get worse. Any more strokes after that simply *prolonged* the agony. You tried not to cry out. Sometimes you couldn't help it. But whether you were able to remain silent or not, it was impossible to stop the tears. They poured down your cheeks in streams and dripped onto the carpet.

The important thing was never to flinch upward or straighten up when you were hit. If you did that, you got an extra one.

Slowly, deliberately, taking plenty of time, the headmaster delivered three more strokes, making six in all.

"You may go." The voice came from a cavern miles away, and you straightened up slowly, agonizingly, and grabbed hold of your burning buttocks with both hands and held them as tight as you could and hopped out of the room on the very tips of your toes.

That cruel cane ruled our lives. We were caned for talking in the dormitory after lights out, for talking in class, for bad work, for carving our initials on the desk, for climbing over walls, for slovenly appearance, for flicking paper clips, for forgetting to change into house-shoes in the evenings, for not hanging up our games clothes, and above all for giving the slightest offense to any master. (They weren't called teachers in those days.) In other words, we were caned for doing everything that it was natural for small boys to do.

So we watched our words. And we watched our steps. My goodness, how we watched our steps. We became incredibly alert. Wherever we went, we walked carefully, with ears pricked for danger, like wild animals stepping softly through the woods.

Apart from the masters, there was another man in the school who frightened us considerably. This was Mr. Pople. Mr. Pople was a paunchy, crimson-faced individual who acted as school porter, boiler superintendent and general handyman. His power stemmed from the fact that he could (and he most certainly did) report us to the headmaster upon the slightest provocation. Mr. Pople's moment of glory came each morning at seven-thirty precisely, when he would stand at the end of the long main corridor and "ring the bell." The bell was huge and made of brass, with a thick wooden handle, and Mr. Pople would swing it back and forth at arm's length in a special way of his own, so that it went *clangetty-clang-clang, clangetty-clang-clang, clangetty-clang-clang*. At the sound of the bell, all the boys in the school, one hundred and eighty of us, would move smartly to our positions in the corridor. We lined up against the walls on both sides and stood stiffly to attention, awaiting the headmaster's inspection.

But at least ten minutes would elapse before the head-master arrived on the scene, and during this time, Mr. Pople would conduct a ceremony so extraordinary that to this day I find it hard to believe it ever took place. There were six lavatories in the school, numbered on their doors from one to six. Mr. Pople, standing at the end of the long corridor, would have in the palm of his hand six small brass disks, each with a number on it, one to six. There was absolute silence as he allowed his eye to travel down the two lines of stiffly standing boys. Then he would bark out a name, "Arkle!"

Arkle would fall out and step briskly down the corridor to where Mr. Pople stood. Mr. Pople would hand him a brass disk. Arkle would then march away toward the lavatories, and to reach them he would have to walk the entire length of the corridor, past all the stationary boys, and then turn left. As soon as he was out of sight, he was allowed to look at his disk and see which lavatory number he had been given.

"Highton!" barked Mr. Pople, and now Highton would fall out to receive his disk and march away.

"Angel!" ... "Williamson!" ... "Gaunt!" ... "Price!" ...

In this manner, six boys selected at Mr. Pople's whim were dispatched to the lavatories to do their duty. Nobody asked them if they might or might not be ready to move their bowels at seven thirty in the morning before breakfast. They were simply ordered to do so. But we considered it a great privilege to be chosen because it meant that during the headmaster's inspection we would be sitting safely out of reach in blessed privacy.

In due course, the headmaster would emerge from his private quarters and take over from Mr. Pople. He walked slowly down one side of the corridor, inspecting each boy with the utmost care, strapping his wristwatch onto his wrist as he went along. The morning inspection was an unnerving experience. Every one of us was terrified of the two sharp brown eyes under their bushy eyebrows as they traveled slowly up and down the length of one's body.

"Go away and brush your hair properly. And don't let it happen again or you'll be sorry."

"Let me see your hands. You have ink on them. Why didn't you wash it off last night?"

"Your tie is crooked, boy. Fall out and tie it again. And do it properly this time."

"I can see mud on that shoe. Didn't I have to talk to you about that last week? Come and see me in my study after breakfast."

And so it went on, the ghastly early morning inspection.

And by the end of it all, when the headmaster had gone away and Mr. Pople started marching us into the dining-room by forms, many of us had lost our appetites for the lumpy porridge that was to come.

I have still got all my school reports from those days more than fifty years ago, and I've gone through them one by one, trying to discover a hint of promise for a future fiction writer. The subject to look at was obviously English Composition. But all my prep school reports under this heading were flat and noncommital, excepting one. The one that took my eye was dated Christmas Term, 1928. I was then twelve, and my English teacher was Mr. Victor Corrado. I remember him vividly, a tall, handsome athlete with black wavy hair and a Roman nose (who one night later on eloped with the matron, Miss Davis, and we never saw either of them again). Anyway, it so happened that Mr. Corrado taught us boxing as well as English composition, and in this particular report it said under English, "See his report on boxing. Precisely the same remarks apply." So we look under Boxing, and there it says, "Too slow and ponderous. His punches are not well-timed and are easily seen coming."

But just once a week at this school, every Saturday morning, every beautiful and blessed Saturday morning, all the shivering horrors would disappear and for two glorious hours I would experience something that came very close to ecstasy.

Unfortunately, this did not happen until one was ten years old. But no matter. Let me try to tell you what it was.

At exactly ten-thirty on Saturday mornings, Mr. Pople's infernal bell would go *clangetty-clang-clang*. This was a signal for the following to take place:

First, all boys of nine and under (about seventy all told) would proceed at once to the large outdoor asphalt

playground behind the main building. Standing on the playground with legs apart and arms folded across her moun-
tainous bosom was Miss Davis, the matron. If it was raining,
the boys were expected to arrive in raincoats. If snowing or
blowing a blizzard, then it was coats and scarves. And school
caps, of course—grey with a red badge on the front—had
always to be worn. But no Act of God, neither tornado nor
hurricane nor volcanic eruption was ever allowed to stop
those ghastly two hour Saturday morning walks that the
seven, eight and nine-year-old little boys had to take along
the windy esplanades of Weston-Super-Mare on Saturday
mornings. They walked in crocodile formation, two by two,
with Miss Davis striding alongside in tweed skirt and
woollen stockings and a felt hat that must surely have been
nibbled by rats.

The other thing that happened when Mr. Pople's bell
rang out on Saturday mornings was that the rest of the
boys, all those of ten and over (about one hundred all told)
would go immediately to the main Assembly Hall and sit
down. A junior master called S. K. Jopp would then poke his
head around the door and shout at us with such ferocity that
specks of spit would fly from his mouth like bullets and
splash against the window panes across the room. "All
right!" he shouted. "No talking! No moving! Eyes front
and hands on desks!" Then out he would pop again.

We sat still and waited. We were waiting for the lovely
time that we knew would be coming soon. Outside in the
driveway we heard the motor-cars being started up. All
were ancient. All had to be cranked by hand. (The year,
don't forget, was around 1927/28). This was a Saturday
morning ritual. There were five cars in all, and into them
would pile the entire staff of fourteen masters, including
not only the headmaster himself but also the purple-faced
Mr. Pople. Then off they would roar in a cloud of blue

smoke and come to rest outside a pub called, if I remember rightly, "The Bewhiskered Earl." There they would remain until just before lunch, drinking pint after pint of strong brown ale. And two and a half hours later, at one o'clock, we would watch them coming back, walking very carefully into the dining-room for lunch, holding onto things as they went by.

So much for the masters. But what of us, the great mass of ten- eleven- and twelve-year-olds left sitting in the Assembly Hall in a school that was suddenly without a single adult in the entire place? We knew, of course, exactly what was going to happen next. Within a minute of the departure of the masters, we would hear the front door opening, and footsteps outside, and then, with a flurry of loose clothes and jangling bracelets and flying hair, a woman would burst into the room shouting, "Hello, everybody! Cheer up! This isn't a burial service!" or words to that effect. And *this* was Mrs. O'Connor.

Blessed beautiful Mrs. O'Connor with her whacky clothes and her grey hair flying in all directions. She was about fifty years old, with a horsey face and long yellow teeth, but to us she was beautiful. She was not on the staff. She was hired from somewhere in the town to come up on Saturday mornings and be a sort of baby sitter, to keep us quiet for two and a half hours while the masters went off boozing at the pub.

But Mrs. O'Connor was no baby sitter. She was nothing less than a great and gifted teacher, a scholar and a lover of English Literature. Each of us was with her every Saturday morning for three years (from the age of ten until we left the school) and during that time we spanned the entire history of English Literature from 597 AD to the early nineteenth century.

Newcomers to the class were given for keeps a slim blue

book called simply "The Chronological Table", and it contained only six pages. Those six pages were filled with a very long list in chronological order of all the great and not so great landmarks in English Literature, together with their dates. Exactly one hundred of these were chosen by Mrs. O'Connor and we marked them in our books and learned them by heart. Here are a few that I still remember:

AD 597   St. Augustine lands in Thanet and brings Christianity to Britain.

731   Bede's *Ecclesiastical History.*

1399   Langland's *Vision concerning Piers Plowman.*

1215   Signing of the Magna Carta

1476   Caxton sets up first printing press at Westminster.

1478   Chaucer's *Canterbury Tales.*

1485   Malory's *Morte d'Arthur.*

1590   Spenser's *Faerie Queene.*

1623   First Folio of Shakespeare.

1667   Milton's *Paradise Lost.*

1668   Dryden's essays.

1678   Bunyan's *Pilgrim's Progress.*

1711   Addison's *Spectator.*

1719   Defoe's *Robinson Crusoe.*

1726   Swift's *Guilliver's Travels.*

1733   Pope's *Essay on Man.*

1755   Johnson's *Dictionary.*

1791   Boswell's *Life of Johnson.*

1833   Carlyle's *Sartor Resartus.*

1859   Darwin's *Origin of Species.*

Mrs. O'Connor would then take each item in turn and spend one entire Saturday morning of two and a half hours talking to us about it. Thus, at the end of three years, with approximately thirty-six Saturdays in each school year, she would have covered the one hundred items.

And what marvelous exciting fun it was! She had the great teacher's knack of making everything she spoke about come alive to us in that room. In two and a half hours, we grew to love Langland and his Piers Plowman. The next Saturday, it was Chaucer, and we loved him, too. Even rather difficult fellows like Milton and Dryden and Pope all became thrilling when Mrs. O'Connor told us about their lives and read parts of their work to us aloud. And the result of all this, for me at any rate, was that by the age of thirteen I had become intensely aware of the vast heritage of literature that had been built up in England over the centuries. I also became an avid and insatiable reader of good writing.

Dear lovely Mrs. O'Connor! Perhaps it was worth going to that awful school simply to experience the joy of her Saturday mornings.

At thirteen I left prep school and was sent, again as a boarder, to one of our famous British public schools. They are not, of course, public at all. They are extremely private and expensive. Mine was called Repton, in Derbyshire, and our headmaster at the time was the Reverend Geoffrey Fisher, who later became Bishop of Chester, then Bishop of London, and finally Archbishop of Canterbury. In his last job, he crowned Queen Elizabeth II in Westminster Abbey.

The clothes we had to wear at this school made us look like assistants in a funeral parlor. Listen to this. The jacket was black, with a cutaway front and long tails hanging down behind that came below the backs of the knees. The trousers were black with thin gray stripes. The shoes were black. There was a black vest with eleven buttons to do up every morning. The tie was black. Then there was a stiff starched white butterfly collar and a white shirt. To top it all off, the final ludicrous touch was a straw hat that had to be worn at all times out-of-doors except when playing games. And because the hats got soggy in the rain, we carried umbrellas for bad weather.

You can imagine what I felt like in this fancy dress when my mother took me at the age of thirteen to the train in London at the beginning of my first term. She kissed me good-bye and off I went.

I naturally hoped that my long-suffering backside would be given a rest at my new and more adult school, but it was not to be. The beatings at Repton were more fierce and more frequent than anything I had yet experienced. And do not think for one moment that the future Archbishop of Canterbury objected to these squalid exercises. He rolled up his sleeves and joined in with gusto. His were the bad ones, the really terrifying occasions. Some of the beatings administered by this man of God, this future Head of the Church of England, were very brutal. To my certain knowledge he once had to produce a basin of water, a sponge and a towel so that the victim could wash the blood away afterwards.

No joke, that.

Shades of the Spanish Inquisition.

But nastiest of all, I think, was the fact that prefects were allowed to beat their fellow pupils. This was a daily occurrence. The big boys (aged 17 or 18) would flog the smaller boys (aged 13, 14, 15) in a sadistic ceremony that took place at night after you had gone up to the dormitory and got into your pajamas.

"You're wanted down in the changing room."

With heavy hands, you would put on your dressing gown and slippers. Then you would stumble downstairs and enter the large wooden-floored room where the games clothes were hanging up around the walls. A single bare electric bulb hung from the ceiling. A prefect, pompous but very dangerous, was waiting for you in the center of the room. In his hands he held a long cane, and he was usually flexing it back and forth as you came in.

"I suppose you know why you're here," he would say.

"Well, I . . ."

"For the second day running you have burnt my toast!"

Let me explain this ludicrous remark. You were this particular prefect's fag. That meant you were his servant, and one of your many duties was to make toast for him every day at teatime. For this, you used a long three-pronged toasting fork, and you stuck the bread on the end of it and held it up before an open fire, first one side, then the other. But the only fire where toasting was allowed was in the library, and as teatime approached, there were never less than a dozen wretched fags all jostling for position in front of the tiny grate. I was no good at this. I usually held it too close and the toast got burnt. But as we were never allowed to ask for a second slice and start again, the only thing to do was to scrape the burnt bits off with a knife. You seldom got away with this. The prefects were expert at detecting scraped toast. You would see your own tormentor sitting up there at the top table, picking up his toast, turning it over, examining it closely as though it were a small and very valuable painting. Then he would frown, and you knew you were for it.

So now it was night-time and you were down in the changing room in your dressing gown and pajamas, and the one whose toast you had burnt was telling you about your crime.

"I don't like burnt toast."

"I held it too close. I'm sorry."

"Which do you want? Four with the dressing gown on, or three with it off."

"Four with it on," I said.

It was traditional to ask this question. The victim was

always given a choice. But my own dressing gown was made of thick brown camel's hair, and there was never any question in my mind that this was the better choice. To be beaten in pajamas only was a very painful experience, and your skin nearly always got broken. But my lovely dressing gown stopped that from happening. The prefect knew, of course, all about this, and therefore whenever you chose to take an extra stroke and kept the dressing gown on, he beat you with every ounce of his strength. Sometimes he would take a little run, three or four neat steps on his toes, to gain momentum and thrust, but either way, it was a savage business.

In the old days, when a man was about to be hanged, a silence would fall upon the whole prison and the other prisoners would sit very quietly in their cells until the deed had been done. Much the same thing happened at school when a beating was taking place. Upstairs in the dormitories, the boys would sit in silence on their beds in sympathy for the victim, and through the silence, from down below in the changing room, would come the *crack* of each stroke as it was delivered.

My end-of-term reports from this school are of considerable interest. Here are just four of them, copied out word for word from the original documents:

Summer Term, 1930 (aged 14). English Composition. "I have never met a boy who so persistently writes the exact opposite of what he means. He seems incapable of marshalling his thoughts on paper."

Easter Term, 1931 (aged 15). English Composition. "A persistent muddler. Vocabulary negligible, sentences mal-constructed. He reminds me of a camel."

Summer Term, 1932 (aged 16). English Composition. "This boy is an indolent and illiterate member of the class."

Autumn Term, 1932 (aged 17). English Composition. "Consistently idle. Ideas limited." (And underneath this one, the future Archbishop of Canterbury had written in red ink, "He must correct the blemishes on this sheet.")

Little wonder that it never entered my head to become a writer in those days.

When I left school at the age of eighteen, in 1934, I turned down my mother's offer (my father died when I was three) to go to university. Unless one was going to become a doctor, a lawyer, a scientist, an engineer or some other kind of professional person, I saw little point in wasting three or four years at Oxford or Cambridge, and I still hold this view. Instead, I had a passionate wish to go abroad, to travel, to see distant lands. Don't forget there were almost no commercial airplanes in those days, and a journey to Africa or the Far East took several weeks.

So I got a job with what was called the Eastern Staff of the Shell Oil Company, where they promised me that after two or three years training in England, I would be sent off to a foreign country.

"Which one?" I asked.

"Who knows?" the man answered. "It depends where there is a vacancy when you reach the top of the list. It could be Egypt or China or India or almost anywhere in the world."

That sounded like fun. It was fun. When my turn came to be posted abroad three years later, I was told it would be East Africa. Tropical suits were ordered, and my mother helped me pack my trunk. My tour of duty was for three years in Africa, then I would be allowed home on leave for six months. I was now twenty-one years old and setting out for faraway places. I felt great. I boarded the ship at London and off she sailed.

That journey took two and a half weeks. We went through the Bay of Biscay and called in at Gibraltar. We headed down the Mediterranean by way of Malta, Naples and Port Said. We went through the Suez Canal and down the Red Sea, stopping at Port Sudan, then Aden. It was all tremendously exciting. For the first time, I saw great sandy deserts, and Arab soldiers mounted on camels, and palm trees with dates growing on them, and flying fish and thousands of other marvelous things. Finally we reached Mombasa, in Kenya.

At Mombasa, a man from the Shell Oil Company came on board and told me I must transfer to a small coastal vessel and go on to Dar-es-Salaam, the capital of Tanganyika (now Tanzania). And so to Dar-es-Salaam I went, stopping at Zanzibar on the way.

For the next two years, I worked for Shell in Tanzania, with my headquarters in Dar-es-Salaam. It was a fantastic life. The heat was intense, but who cared? Our dress was khaki shorts, an open shirt and a topee on the head. I learned to speak Swahili. I drove up-country visiting diamond mines, sisal plantations, gold mines and all the rest of it.

There were giraffes, elephants, zebras, lions and antelopes all over the place, and horrid snakes as well, including the black mamba, which is the only snake in the world that will chase after you if it sees you. And if it catches you and bites you, you had better start saying your prayers. I learned to shake my mosquito boots upside down before putting them on in case there was a scorpion inside, and like everyone else, I got malaria and lay for three days with a temperature of 105.5.

By the summer of 1939, it became obvious that there was going to be a war with Hitler's Germany. Tanganyika, which only twenty years before had been called German East Africa, was still full of Germans. They were everywhere. They owned shops and mines and plantations all over the country. The moment war broke out, they would have to be rounded up. But we had no army to speak of in Tanganyika, only a few native soldiers, known as Askaris, and a handful of officers. So all of us civilian men were made Special Reservists. I was given an armband and put in charge of twenty Askaris. My little troop and I were ordered to block the road that led south out of Tanganyika into neutral Portuguese East Africa. This was an important job, for it was along that road most of the Germans would try to escape when war was declared.

It was exciting to play soldiers like this. I took my happy gang with their rifles and one machine gun and set up a roadblock in a place where the road passed through dense jungle, about ten miles outside the town. We had a field telephone to headquarters, which would tell us at once when war was declared. We settled down to wait. For three days we waited. And during the nights, from all around us in the jungle, came the sound of native drums beating weird hypnotic rhythms. Once, I wandered into the jungle in the dark and came across about fifty natives squatting in a circle around a fire. One man only was beating the drum. Some were dancing around the fire. The remainder were drinking something out of coconut shells. They welcomed me into their circle. They were lovely people. I could talk to them in their language. They gave me a shell filled with a thick gray intoxicating fluid made of fermented maize. It was called, if I remember rightly, pomba. I drank it. It was horrible.

The next afternoon—it was September 3—the field telephone rang and a voice said, "We are at war with Germany." Within minutes, far away in the distance, I saw a line of cars throwing up clouds of dust, heading our way, beating it for the neutral territory of Portuguese East Africa as fast as they could go.

Ho ho, I thought, we are going to have a little battle. And I called out to my twenty Askaris to prepare themselves. But there was no battle. The Germans, who were, after all, only civilian townspeople, saw our machine gun and our rifles and quickly gave themselves up. Within an hour, we had a couple of hundred of them on our hands. I felt rather sorry for them. Many I knew personally, like Willy Hink the watchmaker and Herman Schneider who owned the soda-water factory. Their only crime had been that they were German. But this was war, and in the cool of the evening, we marched them all back to Dar-es-Salaam where they were put into a huge camp surrounded by barbed wire.

The next day, I got into my old car and drove north, heading for Nairobi, in Kenya, to join the RAF. It was a rough trip and it took me four days. Bumpy jungle roads, wide rivers where the car had to be put onto a raft and pulled across by a ferryman hauling on a rope. Long green snakes sliding across the road in front of the car. (Note: Never try to run over a snake because it can be thrown up into the air and may land inside your open car. It's happened many times.) I slept nights in the car. I passed below the beautiful Mount Kilimanjaro, which had a hat of snow on its head. I drove through the Masai country where the men drank cows' blood and every one of them seemed to be seven feet tall. I nearly collided with a giraffe on the Serengeti Plains. But I came safely to Nairobi at last and reported to RAF headquarters at the airport.

For six months, they trained us in small airplanes called Tiger Moths, and those days were also glorious. We skimmed all over Kenya in our little Tiger Moths. We saw great herds of elephant. We saw the pink flamingos on Lake Nakuru. We saw everything there was to see in that magnificent country. And often, before we could take off, we had to chase the zebras off the flying-field. There were twenty of us training to be pilots out there in Nairobi. Seventeen of those twenty were killed during the war.

From Nairobi, they sent us up to Iraq, to a desolate air-force base near Baghdad to finish our training. The place was called Habbanyia, and in the afternoons it got so hot (130 degrees in the shade) that we were not allowed out of our huts. We just lay on the bunks and sweated. The un-lucky ones got heatstroke and were taken to the hospital and packed in ice for several days. This either killed them or saved them. It was a fifty-fifty chance.

At Habbanyia, they taught us to fly more powerful air-planes with guns in them, and we practiced shooting at targets in the air (drogues pulled behind other planes) and at objects on the ground.

Finally, our training was finished, and we were sent to Egypt to fight against the Italians in the Western Desert of Libya. I joined 80 Squadron, which flew fighters, and at first we had only ancient single-seater biplanes called Glos-ter Gladiators. The two machine-guns on a Gladiator were mounted one on either side of the engine, and they fired their bullets, believe it or not, *through* the propeller. The guns were somehow synchronized with the propeller shaft so that in theory the bullets missed the whirling propeller blades. But as you might guess, this complicated mechanism often went wrong, and the poor pilot, who was trying to shoot down the enemy, shot off his own propeller instead.

I myself was shot down in a Gladiator that crashed far out in the Libyan desert between the enemy lines. The plane burst into flames, but I managed to get out and was finally rescued and carried back to safety by our own soldiers, who crawled out across the sand under cover of darkness.

That crash sent me to the hospital in Alexandria for six months with a fractured skull and a lot of burns. When I came out, in April 1941, my squadron had been moved to Greece to fight the Germans who were invading from the north. I was given a Hurricane and told to fly it from Egypt to Greece and join the squadron. Now, a Hurricane fighter was not at all like the old Gladiator. It had eight Browning machine-guns, four in each wing, and all eight of them fired simultaneously when you pressed the small button on your joystick. It was a magnificent plane, but it had a range of only two hours flying time. The journey to Greece, nonstop, would take nearly five hours, always over the water. They put extra fuel-tanks on the wings. They said I would make it. In the end, I did. But only just. And I can promise you that when you are six feet six inches tall, as I am, it is no joke to be sitting crunched up in a tiny cockpit for five hours.

In Greece, the RAF had a total of about eighteen Hurricanes. The Germans had at least one thousand airplanes to operate with. We had a hard time. We were driven from our airfield outside Athens (Elevsis), and flew for a while from a small secret landing strip farther west (Megara). The Germans soon found that one and bashed it to bits, so with the few planes we had left, we flew off to a tiny field (Argos) right down in the south of Greece, where we hid our Hurricanes under the olive trees when we weren't flying.

But this couldn't last long. Soon, we had only five Hurricanes left, and not many pilots still alive. Those five planes were flown to the island of Crete. The Germans captured Crete. Some of us escaped. I was one of the lucky ones. I finished up back in Egypt. The squadron was reformed and again equipped with Hurricanes. We were sent off to Haifa, which was then in Palestine (now Israel), where we fought the Germans again and the Vichy French in Lebanon and Syria.

At that point, my old head injuries caught up with me. Severe headaches compelled me to stop flying. I was invalided back to England and sailed on a troopship from Suez to Durban to Capetown to Lagos to Liverpool, chased by German submarines in the Atlantic and bombed by long-range Focke-Wulf aircraft every day for the last week of the voyage.

I had been away from home for four years. My mother, bombed out of her house in Kent during the Battle of Britain and now living in a small thatched cottage in Buckinghamshire, was happy to see me. So were my four sisters and my brother. I was given a month's leave. Then suddenly I was told I was being sent to Washington, D.C., in the United States of America as assistant air attaché. This was January 1942, and one month earlier the Japanese had bombed the American fleet in Pearl Harbor. So the United States was now in the war as well.

I was twenty-six years old when I arrived in Washington, and I still had no thoughts of becoming a writer.

During the morning of my third day, I was sitting in my new office at the British Embassy and wondering what on earth I was meant to be doing when there was a knock on my door. "Come in."

A very small man with thick steel-rimmed spectacles shuffled shyly into the room. "Forgive me for bothering you," he said.

"You aren't bothering me at all," I answered. "I'm not doing a thing."

He stood before me looking very uncomfortable and out of place. I thought perhaps he was going to ask for a job.

"My name," he said, "is Forester. C. S. Forester."

I nearly fell out of my chair. "Are you joking?" I said.

"No," he said, smiling. "That's me."

And it was. It was the great writer himself, the inventor of Captain Hornblower and the best teller of tales about the sea since Joseph Conrad. I asked him to take a seat.

"Look," he said. "I'm too old for the war. I live over here now. The only thing I can do to help is to write things about Britain for the American papers and magazines. We need all the help America can give us. A magazine called the *Saturday Evening Post* will publish any story I write. I have a contract with them. And I have come to you because I think you might have a good story to tell. I mean about flying."

"No more than thousands of others," I said. "There are lots of pilots who have shot down many more planes than me."

"That's not the point," Forester said. "You are now in America, and because you have, as they say over here, 'been in combat,' you are a rare bird on this side of the Atlantic. Don't forget they have only just entered the war."

"What do you want me to do?" I asked.

"Come and have lunch with me," he said. "And while we're eating, you can tell me all about it. Tell me your most exciting adventure and I'll write it up for the *Saturday Evening Post*. Every little bit helps."

I was thrilled. I had never met a famous writer before. I examined him closely as he sat in my office. What astonished me was that he looked so ordinary. There was nothing in the least unusual about him. His face, his conversation, his eyes behind the spectacles, even his clothes were all exceedingly normal. And yet here was a writer of stories who was famous the world over. His books had been read by millions of people. I expected sparks to be shooting out of his head, or at the very least, he should have been wearing a long green cloak and a floppy hat with a wide brim.

But no. And it was then I began to realize for the first time that there are two distinct sides to a writer of fiction. First, there is the side he displays to the public, that of an ordinary person like anyone else, a person who does ordinary things and speaks an ordinary language. Second, there is the secret side, which comes out in him only after he has closed the door of his workroom and is completely alone. It is then that he slips into another world altogether, a world where his imagination takes over and he finds himself actually *living* in the places he is writing about at that moment. I myself, if you want to know, fall into a kind of trance, and everything around me disappears. I see only the point of my pencil moving over the paper, and quite often two hours go by as though they were a couple of seconds.

"Come along," C. S. Forester said to me. "Let's go to lunch. You don't seem to have anything else to do."

As I walked out of the embassy side by side with the great man, I was churning with excitement. I had read all the Hornblowers and just about everything else he had written. I had, and still have, a great love for books about the sea. I had read all of Conrad and all of that other splendid sea writer, Captain Marryat (*Mr. Midshipman Easy, From Powder Monkey to Admiral,* etc.), and now here I was about to have lunch with somebody who, to my mind, was also pretty terrific.

He took me to a small expensive French restaurant somewhere near the Mayflower Hotel in Washington. He ordered a sumptuous lunch, then he produced a small notebook and a pencil (ballpoint pens had not been invented in 1942) and laid them on the tablecloth. "Now," he said, "tell me about the most exciting or frightening or dangerous thing that happened to you when you were flying fighter planes."

I tried to get going. I was telling him about the time I

was shot down in the Western Desert and the plane had burst into flames.

The waitress brought two plates of smoked salmon. While we tried to eat it, I was trying to talk and Forester was trying to take notes.

The main course was roast duck with vegetables and potatoes and a thick rich gravy. This was a dish that required one's full attention as well as two hands. My narrative began to flounder. Forester kept putting down the pencil and picking up the fork and vice versa. Things weren't going well. And apart from that, I have never been much good at telling stories aloud.

"Look," I said. "If you like I'll try to write down on paper what happened and send it to you. Then you can rewrite it properly yourself in your own time. Wouldn't that be easier? I could do it tonight."

That, though I didn't know it at the time, was the moment that changed my life.

"A splendid idea," Forester said. "Then I can put this silly notebook away and we can enjoy our lunch. Would you really mind doing that for me?"

"I don't mind a bit," I said. "But you mustn't expect it to be any good. I'll just put down the facts."

"Don't worry," he said. "As long as the facts are there, I can write the story. But please," he added, "let me have plenty of detail. That's what counts in our business, tiny little details, like you had a broken shoelace on your left shoe or a fly settled on the rim of your glass at lunch or the man you were talking to had a broken front tooth. Try to think back and remember everything."

"I'll do my best," I said.

He gave me an address where I could send the story, and then we forgot all about it and finished our lunch at leisure. But Mr. Forester was not a great talker. He certainly couldn't talk the way he wrote, and although he was kind and gentle, no sparks ever flew out of his head and I might just as well have been talking to an intelligent stockbroker or a lawyer.

That night, in the small house I lived in alone in a suburb of Washington, I sat down and wrote my story. I started at about seven o'clock and finished at midnight. I remember I had a glass of Portuguese brandy to keep me going. For the first time in my life, I became totally absorbed in what I was doing. I floated back in time and once again I was in the sizzling hot desert of Libya, with white sand underfoot, climbing up into the cockpit of the old Gladiator, strapping myself in, adjusting my helmet, starting the motor and taxiing out for takeoff. It was astonishing how everything came back to me with absolute clarity. Writing it down on paper was not difficult. The story seemed to be telling itself, and the hand that held the pencil moved rapidly back and forth across each page. Just for fun, when it was finished, I gave it a title. I called it "A Piece of Cake."*

The next day, somebody in the embassy typed it out for me, and I sent it off to Mr. Forester. Then I forgot all about it.

Exactly two weeks later, I received a reply from the great man. It said:

> *Dear RD, You were meant to give me notes, not a finished story. I'm bowled over. Your piece is marvellous. It is the work of a gifted writer. I didn't touch a word of it. I sent it at once under your name to my agent, Harold Matson, asking him to offer it to the* Saturday Evening Post *with my per-*

---

* "A Piece of Cake" is reprinted at the end of this book.

sonal recommendation. You will be happy to hear that the Post *accepted it immediately and have paid one thousand dollars. Mr. Matson's commission is ten percent. I enclose his check for nine hundred dollars. It's all yours. As you will see from Mr. Matson's letter, which I also enclose, the* Post *is asking if you will write more stories for them. I do hope you will. Did you know you were a writer? With my very best wishes and congratulations, C. S. Forester.*

Well! I thought. My goodness me! Nine hundred dollars! And they're going to print it! But surely it can't be as easy as all that.

Oddly enough, it was.

The next story I wrote was fiction. I made it up. Don't ask me why. And Mr. Matson sold that one, too. Out there in Washington in the evenings over the next two years, I wrote eleven short stories. All were sold to American magazines, and later they were published in a little book called *Over to You.*

Early on in this period, I also had a go at a story for children. It was called "The Gremlins," and this I believe was the first time the word had been used. In my story, Gremlins were tiny men who lived on RAF fighter planes and bombers, and it was the Gremlins, not the enemy, who were responsible for all the bullet holes and burning engines and crashes that took place during combat. The Gremlins had wives called Fifinellas, and children called Widgets, and although the story itself was clearly the work of an inexperienced writer, it was bought by Walt Disney, who decided he was going to make it into a full-length animated film. But first it was published in *Cosmopolitan* magazine with Disney's colored illustrations (December 1942), and

from then on, news of the Gremlins spread rapidly through
the whole of the RAF and the United States Air Force, and
they became something of a legend.

Because of the Gremlins, I was given three weeks leave
from my duties at the embassy in Washington and whisked
out to Hollywood. There I was put up at Disney's expense in
a luxurious Beverly Hills hotel and given a huge shiny car
to drive about in. Each day, I worked with the great Disney
at his studios in Burbank, roughing out the story line for
the forthcoming film. I had a ball. I was still only twenty-
six. I attended story conferences in Disney's enormous office
where every word spoken, every suggestion made, was taken
down by a stenographer and typed out afterward. I mooched
around the rooms where the gifted and obstreperous anima-
tors worked, the men who had already created *Snow White,
Dumbo, Bambi* and other marvelous films, and in those days,
as long as these crazy artists did their work, Disney didn't
care when they turned up at the studio or how they behaved.

When my time was up, I went back to Washington and
left them to it.

My Gremlin story was also published as a children's book
in New York and London, full of Disney's color illustrations,
and it was called of course *The Gremlins*. Copies are very
scarce now and hard to come by. I myself have only one. The
film, alas, was never finished. I have a feeling that Disney
was not really very comfortable with this particular fan-
tasy. Out there in Hollywood, he was a long way away from
the great war in the air that was going on in Europe. Furthermore, it was a story about the Royal Air Force and not
about his own countrymen, and that, I think, added to his
sense of bewilderment. So in the end, he lost interest and
dropped the whole idea.

My little Gremlin book caused something else quite extraordinary to happen to me in those wartime Washington

days. Eleanor Roosevelt read it to her grandchildren in the
White House and was apparently much taken with it. I was
invited to dinner with her and the President. I went, shaking with excitement. We had a splendid time, and I was
invited again. Then Mrs. Roosevelt began asking me for
weekends to Hyde Park, the President's country house. Up
there, believe it or not, I spent a good deal of time alone
with Franklin Roosevelt during his relaxing hours. I would
sit with him while he mixed the martinis before Sunday
lunch, and he would say things like, "I've just had an interesting cable from Mr. Churchill." Then he would tell me
what it said, something perhaps about new plans for the
bombing of Germany or the sinking of U-boats, and I would
do my best to appear calm and chatty, though actually I
was trembling at the realization that the most powerful man
in the world was telling me these mighty secrets. Sometimes
he drove me around the estate in his car, an old Ford, I
think it was, that had been specially adapted for his para-
lyzed legs. It had no pedals. All the controls were worked by
his hands. His secret-service men would lift him out of his
wheelchair into the driver's seat, then he would wave them
away and off we would go, driving at terrific speeds along
the narrow roads.

One Sunday during lunch at Hyde Park, Franklin Roosevelt told a story that shook the assembled guests. There
were about fourteen of us sitting on both sides of the long
dining-room table, including Princess Martha of Norway
and several members of the Cabinet. We were eating a
rather insipid white fish covered with a thick gray sauce.
Suddenly the President pointed a finger at me and said, "We
have an Englishman here. Let me tell you what happened to
another Englishman, a representative of the King, who was
in Washington in the year 1827." He gave the man's name,
but I've forgotten it. Then he went on, "While he was over

here, this fellow died, and the British for some reason insisted that his body be sent home to England for burial. Now the only way to do that in those days was to pickle it in alcohol. So the body was put into a barrel of rum. The barrel was lashed to the mast of a schooner and the ship sailed for home. After about four weeks at sea, the captain of the schooner noticed a most frightful stench coming from the barrel. And in the end, the smell became so appalling they had to cut the barrel loose and roll it overboard. But do you know *why* it stank so badly?" the President asked, beaming at the guests with that famous wide smile of his. "I will tell you exactly why. Some of the sailors had drilled a hole in the bottom of the barrel and had inserted a bung. Then every night they had been helping themselves to the rum. And when they had drunk it all, that's when the trouble started." Franklin Roosevelt let out a great roar of laughter. Several females at the table turned very pale and I saw them pushing their plates of boiled white fish gently away.

All the stories I wrote in those early days were fiction, except for the first one I did with C. S. Forester. Nonfiction, which means writing about things that have actually taken place, doesn't interest me. I enjoy least of all writing about my own experiences. And that explains why this particular story is so lacking in detail. I could easily have described what it was like to be in a dogfight with German fighters fifteen thousand feet above the Parthenon in Athens, or the thrill of chasing a Junkers 88 in and out the mountain peaks in northern Greece, but I don't want to do it. For me, the pleasure of writing comes with inventing stories.

Apart from the Forester story, I think I have written only one other nonfiction piece in my life, and I did this only because the subject was so enthralling I couldn't resist it. The story is called "The Mildenhall Treasure," and you'll find it in this book.

So there you are. That's how I became a writer. Had I
not been lucky enough to meet Mr. Forester, it would probably never have happened.

Now, more than thirty years later, I'm still slogging
away. To me, the most important and difficult thing about
writing fiction is to find the plot. Good original plots are
very hard to come by. You never know when a lovely idea is
going to flit suddenly into your mind, but by golly, when it
does come along, you grab it with both hands and hang on to
it tight. The trick is to write it down at once, otherwise
you'll forget it. A good plot is like a dream. If you don't
write down your dream on paper the moment you wake up,
the chances are you'll forget it, and it'll be gone forever.

So when an idea for a story comes popping into my mind,
I rush for a pencil, a crayon, a lipstick, anything that will
write, and scribble a few words that will later remind me
of the idea. Often, one word is enough. I was once driving
alone on a country road and an idea came for a story about
someone getting stuck in an elevator between two floors
in an empty house. I had nothing to write with in the
car. So I stopped and got out. The back of the car was
covered with dust. With one finger I wrote in the dust the
single word ELEVATOR. That was enough. As soon as I got
home, I went straight to my workroom and wrote the idea
down in an old school exercise book that is simply labeled
Short Stories.

I have had this book ever since I started trying to write
seriously. There are ninety-eight pages in the book. I've
counted them. And just about every one of those pages is
filled up on both sides with these so-called story ideas. Many
are no good. But just about every story and every children's
book I have ever written has started out as a three- or four-
line note in this little, much-worn, red-covered volume. For
example:

What about a chocolate factory
That makes marvellous and fantastic
Things — with a crazy man running it?

This became CHARLIE AND THE CHOCOLATE FACTORY.

A story about Mr. Fox who has
a whole network of underground
Tunnels. They lead to all the shops in
the village. At night he goes up
Through the floorboards and helps himself.

FANTASTIC MR. FOX.

Jamaica and the small boy who
saw a giant Turtle captured by
native fishermen. Boy pleads with
his father to buy Turtle and release
it. Becomes hysterical. Father buys
it. Then what? Perhaps boy goes
with Turtle.

THE BOY WHO TALKED WITH ANIMALS

A man acquires the ability to see through playing-cards. He makes millions at casinos.

THE WONDERFUL STORY OF HENRY SUGAR

Sometimes, these little scribbles stay unused in the note-book for five or even ten years. But the promising ones are always used in the end. And if they show nothing else, they do, I think, demonstrate from what slender threads a children's book or a short story must ultimately be woven. The story builds and expands while you are writing it. All the best stuff comes at the desk. But you can't even start to write that story unless you have the beginnings of a plot. Without my little notebook, I would be quite helpless.

A Piece of Cake

First Story-1942

I do not remember much of it; not beforehand anyway; not until it happened.

There was the landing at Fouka, where the Blenheim boys were helpful and gave us tea while we
were being refuelled. I remember the quietness of the
Blenheim boys, how they came into the mess-tent to
get some tea and sat down to drink it without saying
anything; how they got up and went out when they
had finished drinking and still they did not say anything. And I knew that each one was holding himself
together because the going was not very good right
then. They were having to go out too often, and there
were no replacements coming along.

We thanked them for the tea and went out to see if
they had finished refueling our Gladiators. I remember that there was a wind blowing which made the
windsock stand out straight, like a signpost, and the
sand was blowing up around our legs and making a
rustling noise as it swished against the tents, and the
tents flapped in the wind so that they were like canvas
men clapping their hands.

"Bomber boys unhappy," Peter said.

"Not unhappy," I answered.

"Well, they're browned off."

"No. They've had it, that's all. But they'll keep going. You can see they're trying to keep going."

Our two old Gladiators were standing beside each other in the sand and the airmen in their khaki shirts and shorts seemed still to be busy with the refueling. I was wearing a thin white cotton flying suit and Peter had on a blue one. It wasn't necessary to fly with anything warmer.

Peter said, "How far away is it?"

"Twenty-one miles beyond Charing Cross," I answered, "on the right side of the road." Charing Cross was where the desert road branched north to Mersah Matruh. The Italian army was outside Mersah, and they were doing pretty well. It was about the only time, so far as I know, that the Italians have done pretty well. Their morale goes up and down like a sensitive altimeter, and right then it was at forty thousand because the Axis was on top of the world. We hung around waiting for the refueling to finish.

Peter said, "It's a piece of cake."

"Yes. It ought to be easy."

We separated and I climbed into my cockpit. I have always remembered the face of the airman who helped me to strap in. He was oldish, about forty, and bald except for a neat patch of golden hair at the back of his head. His face was all wrinkles, his eyes were like my grandmother's eyes, and he looked as though he had spent his life helping to strap in pilots who never came back. He stood on the wing pulling my straps and said, "Be careful. There isn't any sense not being careful."

"Piece of cake," I said.

"Like hell."

"Really. It isn't anything at all. It's a piece of cake."

I don't remember much about the next bit; I only remember about later on. I suppose we took off from Fouka and flew west toward Mersah, and I suppose we flew at about eight hundred feet. I suppose we saw the sea to starboard, and I suppose—no, I am certain —that it was blue and that it was beautiful, especially where it rolled up onto the sand and made a long thick white line east and west as far as you could see. I suppose we flew over Charing Cross and flew on for twenty-one miles to where they had said it would be, but I do not know. I know only that there was trouble, lots and lots of trouble, and I know that we had turned round and were coming back when the trouble got worse. The biggest trouble of all was that I was too low to bail out, and it is from that point on that my memory comes back to me. I remember the dipping of the nose of the aircraft and I remember looking down the nose of the machine at the ground and seeing a little clump of camel-thorn growing there all by itself. I remember seeing some rocks lying in the sand beside the camel-thorn, and the camel-thorn and the sand and the rocks leapt out of the ground and came to me. I remember that very clearly.

Then there was a small gap of not-remembering. It might have been one second or it might have been thirty; I do not know. I have an idea that it was very short, a second perhaps, and next I heard a *crumph* on the right as the starboard wing tank caught fire, then another *crumph* on the left as the port tank did the same. To me that was not significant, and for a while I sat still, feeling comfortable, but a little drowsy. I couldn't see with my eyes, but that was not

significant either. There was nothing to worry about.
Nothing at all. Not until I felt the hotness around my
legs. At first it was only a warmness and that was all
right too, but all at once it was a hotness, a very sting-
ing scorching hotness up and down the sides of each
leg.

I knew that the hotness was unpleasant, but that
was all I knew. I disliked it, so I curled my legs up
under the seat and waited. I think there was something wrong with the telegraph system between the
body and the brain. It did not seem to be working
very well. Somehow it was a bit slow in telling the
brain all about it and in asking for instructions. But I
believe a message eventually got through, saying,
"Down here there is great hotness. What shall we do?
(Signed) Left Leg and Right Leg." For a long time
there was no reply. The brain was figuring the matter
out.

Then slowly, word by word, the answer was tapped
over the wires. "The plane—is—burning. Get—out
—repeat—get—out—get—out." The order was re-
layed to the whole system, to all the muscles in the
legs, arms and body, and the muscles went to work.
They tried their best; they pushed a little and pulled
a little, and they strained greatly, but it wasn't any
good. Up went another telegram, "Can't get out. Something holding us in." The answer to this one took even
longer in arriving, so I just sat there waiting for it to
come, and all the time the hotness increased. Something was holding me down and it was up to the brain
to find out what it was. Was it giants' hands pressing
on my shoulders, or heavy stones or houses or steam

rollers or filing cabinets or gravity or was it ropes? Wait a minute. Ropes—ropes. The message was beginning to come through. It came very slowly. "Your—straps. Undo—your—straps." My arms received the message and went to work. They tugged at the straps, but they wouldn't undo. They tugged again and again, a little feebly, but as hard as they could, and it wasn't any use. Back went the message, "How do we undo the straps?"

This time I think that I sat there for three or four minutes waiting for the answer. It wasn't any use hurrying or getting impatient. That was the one thing of which I was sure. But what a long time it was all taking. I said aloud. "Bugger it. I'm going to be burnt. I'm . . ." but I was interrupted. The answer was coming—no, it wasn't—yes, it was, it was slowly coming through. "Pull—out—the—quick—release—pin—you—bloody—fool—and—hurry."

Out came the pin and the straps were loosed. Now, let's get out. Let's get out, let's get out. But I couldn't do it. I simply lift myself out of the cockpit. Arms and legs tried their best but it wasn't any use. A last desperate message was flashed upwards and this time it was marked "Urgent." Something else is holding us down," it said. "Something else, something else, something heavy."

Still the arms and legs did not fight. They seemed to know instinctively that there was no point in using up their strength. They stayed quiet and waited for the answer, and oh what a time it took. Twenty, thirty, forty hot seconds. None of them really white hot yet, no sizzling of flesh or smell of burning meat, but that would come any moment now, because those old Gladiators aren't made of stressed steel like a Hurricane or a Spit. They have taut canvas wings, covered with magnificently inflammable dope, and underneath there are hundreds of small thin sticks, the kind you put under the logs for kindling, only these are drier and thinner. If a clever man said, "I am going to build a big thing that will burn better and quicker than anything else in the world," and if he applied himself diligently to his task, he would probably finish up by building something very like a Gladiator. I sat still waiting.

Then suddenly the reply, beautiful in its briefness, but at the same time explaining everything. "Your—parachute—turn—the—buckle."

I turned the buckle, released the parachute harness and with some effort hoisted myself up and tumbled over the side of the cockpit. Something seemed to be burning, so I rolled about a bit in the sand, then crawled away from the fire on all fours and lay down.

I heard some of my machine-gun ammunition going off in the heat and I heard some of the bullets thumping into the sand nearby. I did not worry about them; I merely heard them.

Things were beginning to hurt. My face hurt most. There was something wrong with my face. Something had happened to it. Slowly I put up a hand to feel it. It was sticky. My nose didn't seem to be there. I tried to feel my teeth, but I cannot remember whether I came to any conclusion about them. I think I dozed off.

All of a sudden there was Peter. I heard his voice

and I heard him dancing around and yelling like a madman and shaking my hand and saying. "Jesus, I thought you were still inside. I came down half a mile away and ran like hell. Are you all right?"

I said, "Peter, what has happened to my nose?"

I heard him striking a match in the dark. The night comes quickly in the desert. There was a pause.

"It actually doesn't seem to be there very much," he said. "Does it hurt?"

"Don't be a bloody fool, of course it hurts."

He said he was going back to his machine to get some morphia out of his emergency pack, but he came back again soon, saying he couldn't find his aircraft in the dark.

"Peter," I said, "I can't see anything."

"It's night," he answered. "I can't see either. Don't worry about that."

It was cold now. It was bitter cold, and Peter lay down close alongside so that we could both keep a little warmer. Every now and then he would say, "I've never seen a man without a nose before." I kept spewing a lot of blood and every time I did it, Peter lit a match. Once he gave me a cigarette, but it got wet and I didn't want it anyway.

I do not know how long we stayed there and I remember only very little more. I remember that I kept telling Peter that there was a tin of sore throat tablets in my pocket, and that he should take one, otherwise he would catch my sore throat. I remember asking him where we were and him saying. "We're between the two armies," and then I remember English voices from an English patrol asking if we were Italians.

Peter said something to them; I cannot remember what he said.

Later I remember hot thick soup and one spoonful making me sick. And all the time the pleasant feeling that Peter was around, being wonderful, doing wonderful little things and never going away. That is all that I can remember.

The men stood beside the airplane painting away and talking about the heat.

"Painting pictures on the aircraft," I said.

"Yes," said Peter. "It's a great idea. It's subtle."

"Why?" I said. "Just you tell me."

"They're funny pictures," he said. "The German pilots will all laugh when they see them; they'll shake so with their laughing that they won't be able to shoot straight."

"Oh baloney baloney baloney."

"No, it's a great idea. It's fine. Come and have a look."

We ran towards the line of aircraft. "Hop, skip, jump," said Peter. "Hop skip jump, keep in time."

"Hop skip jump," I said, "Hop skip jump," and we danced along.

The painter on the first airplane had a straw hat on his head and a sad face. He was copying the drawing out of a magazine, and when Peter saw it he said, "Boy oh boy look at that picture," he began to laugh. His laugh began with a rumble and grew quickly into a belly-roar and he slapped his thighs with his hands both at the same time and went on laughing with his body doubled up and his mouth wide open and his eyes shut. His silk top hat fell off his head onto the sand.

"That's not funny," I said.

"Not funny!" he cried. "What d'you mean 'not funny'? Look at me. Look at me laughing. Laughing like this I couldn't hit anything. I couldn't hit a hay wagon or a house or a louse." And he capered about on the sand, gurgling and shaking with laughter. Then he seized me by the arm and we danced over to the next airplane. "Hop skip jump," he said. "Hop skip jump."

There was a small man with a crumpled face writing a long story on the fuselage with a red crayon. His straw hat was perched right on the back of his head and his face was shiny with sweat.

"Good morning," he said. "Good morning, good morning," and he swept his hat off his head in a very elegant way.

Peter said, "Shut up," and bent down and began to read what the little man had been writing. All the time Peter was spluttering and rumbling with laughter, and as he read he began to laugh afresh. He rocked from one side to the other and danced around on the sand slapping his thighs with his hands and bending his body. "Oh my, what a story, what a story, what a story. Look at me. Look at me laughing," and he hopped about on his toes, shaking his head and chortling like a madman. Then suddenly I saw the joke and I began to laugh with him. I laughed so much that my stomach hurt and I fell down and rolled around on the sand and roared and roared because it was so funny that there was nothing else I could do.

"Peter, you're marvelous," I shouted. "But can all those German pilots read English?"

"Oh hell," he said. "Oh hell. Stop," he shouted. "Stop your work," and the painters all stopped their painting and turned round slowly and looked at Peter. They did a little caper on their toes and began to chant in unison. "Rubbishy things—on all the wings, on all the wings, on all the wings," they chanted.

"Shut up," said Peter. "We're in a jam. We must keep calm. Where's my top hat?"

"What?" I said.

"You can speak German," he said. "You must translate for us. He will translate for you," he shouted to the painters. "He will translate."

Then I saw his black top hat lying in the sand. I looked away, then I looked around and saw it again. It was a silk opera hat and it was lying there on its side in the sand.

"You're mad," I shouted. "You're madder than hell. You don't know what you're doing. You'll get us all killed. You're absolutely plumb crazy, do you know that? You're crazier than hell. My God, you're crazy."

"Goodness, what a noise you're making. You mustn't shout like that; it's not good for you." This was a woman's voice. "You've made yourself all hot," she said, and I felt someone wiping my forehead with a handkerchief. "You mustn't work yourself up like that."

Then she was gone and I saw only the sky, which was pale blue. There were no clouds and all around were the German fighters. They were above, below and on every side and there was no way I could go; there was nothing I could do. They took it in turns to come in to attack and they flew their aircraft carelessly, banking and looping and dancing in the air. But I was not frightened, because of the funny pictures on my wings. I was confident and I thought, "I am going to fight a hundred of them alone and I'll shoot them all down. I'll shoot them while they are laughing; that's what I'll do."

Then they flew closer. The whole sky was full of them. There were so many that I did not know which ones to watch and which ones to attack. There were so many that they made a black curtain over the sky and only here and there could I see a little of the blue showing through. But there was enough to patch a Dutchman's trousers, which was all that mattered. So long as there was enough to do that, then everything was all right.

Still they flew closer. They came nearer and nearer, right up in front of my face so that I saw only the black crosses which stood out brightly against the color of the Messerschmitts and against the blue of the sky; and as I turned my head quickly from one side to the other I saw more aircraft and more crosses and then I saw nothing but the arms of the crosses and the blue of the sky. The arms had hands and they joined together and made a circle and danced around my Gladiator, while the engines of the Messerschmitts sang joyfully in a deep voice. They were playing "Oranges and Lemons" and every now and then two would detach themselves and come out into the middle of the floor and make an attack and I knew then that it was "Oranges and Lemons." They banked and swerved and danced upon their toes and they leant against the air first to one side, then to the other. "Oranges and Lemons said the bells of St. Clements," sang the engines.

But I was still confident. I could dance better than they and I had a better partner. She was the most beautiful girl in the world. I looked down and I saw the curve of her neck and the gentle slope of her pale shoulders and I saw her slender arms, eager and outstretched.

Suddenly I saw some bullet holes in my starboard wing and I got angry and scared both at the same time; but mostly I got angry. Then I got confident and I said, "The German who did that had no sense of humor. There's always one man in a party who has no sense of humor. But there's nothing to worry about; there's nothing at all to worry about."

Then I saw more bullet holes and I got scared. I slid back the hood of the cockpit and stood up and shouted, "You fools, look at the funny pictures. Look at the one on my tail; look at the story on my fuselage. Please look at the story on my fuselage."

But they kept on coming. They tripped into the middle of the floor in twos, shooting at me as they came. And the engines of the Messerschmitts sang loudly. "When will you pay me, said the bells of Old Bailey?" sang the engines, and as they sang the black crosses danced and swayed to the rhythm of the music. There were more holes in my wings, in the engine cowling and in the cockpit.

Then suddenly there were some in my body.

But there was no pain, even when I went into a spin, when the wings of my plane went flip, flip, flip flip, faster and faster, when the blue sky and the black sea chased each other round and round until there was no longer any sky or sea but just the flashing of the sun as I turned. But the black crosses were following me down, still dancing and still holding hands and I could still hear the singing of their engines. "Here comes a candle to light you to bed, here comes a chopper to chop off your head," sang the engines.

Still the wings went flip flip, flip flip, and there was neither sky nor sea around me, but only the sun.

Then there was only the sea. I could see it below me and I could see the white horses, and I said to myself, "Those are white horses riding a rough sea." I knew then that my brain was going well because of the white horses and because of the sea. I knew that there was not much time because the sea and the white horses were nearer, the white horses were bigger and the sea was like a sea and like water, not like a smooth plate. Then there was only one white horse, rushing forward madly with his bit in his teeth, foaming at the mouth, scattering the spray with his hooves and arching his neck as he ran. He galloped on madly over the sea, riderless and uncontrollable, and I could tell that we were going to crash.

After that it was warmer, and there were no black crosses and there was no sky. But it was only warm because it was not hot and it was not cold. I was sitting in a great red chair made of velvet and it was evening. There was a wind blowing from behind.

"Where am I?" I said.

"You are missing. You are missing, believed
killed."

"Then I must tell my mother."

"You can't. You can't use that phone."

"Why not?"

"It goes only to God."

"What did you say I was?"

"Missing, believed killed."

"That's not true. It's a lie. It's a lousy lie because
here I am and I'm not missing. You're just trying to
frighten me and you won't succeed. You won't succeed, I tell you, because I know it's a lie and I'm
going back to my squadron. You can't stop me because
I'll just go. I'm going, you see, I'm going."

I got up from the red chair and began to run.

"Let me see those X-rays again, nurse."

"They're here, doctor." This was the woman's voice
again, and now it came closer. "You have been making a noise tonight, haven't you? Let me straighten
your pillow for you, you're pushing it onto the floor."
The voice was close and it was very soft and nice.

"Am I missing?"

"No, of course not. You're fine."

"They said I was missing."

"Don't be silly; you're fine."

Oh everyone's silly, silly, silly, but it was a lovely
day, and I did not want to run but I couldn't stop. I
kept on running across the grass and I couldn't stop
because my legs were carrying me and I had no control over them. It was as if they did not belong to me,
although when I looked down I saw that they were
mine, that the shoes on the feet were mine and that

the legs were joined to my body. But they would not do what I wanted; they just went on running across the field and I had to go with them. I ran and ran and ran, and although in some places the field was rough and bumpy, I never stumbled. I ran past trees and hedges and in one field there were some sheep which stopped their eating and scampered off as I ran past them. Once I saw my Mother in a pale gray dress bending down picking mushrooms, and as I ran past she looked up and said, "My basket's nearly full; shall we go home soon?" but my legs wouldn't stop and I had to go on.

Then I saw the cliff ahead and I saw how dark it was beyond the cliff. There was this great cliff and beyond it there was nothing but darkness, although the sun was shining in the field where I was running. The light of the sun stopped dead at the edge of the cliff and there was only darkness beyond. "That must be where the night begins," I thought, and once more I tried to stop but it was not any good. My legs began to go faster toward the cliff and they began to take longer strides, and I reached down with my hand and tried to stop them by clutching the cloth of my trousers, but it did not work; then I tried to fall down. But my legs were nimble, and each time I threw myself to the ground I landed on my toes and went on running.

Now the cliff and the darkness were much nearer and I could see that unless I stopped quickly I should go over the edge. Once more I tried to throw myself to the ground and once more I landed on my toes and went on running.

I was going fast as I came to the edge and I went straight on over it into the darkness and began to fall.

At first it was not quite dark. I could see little trees growing out of the face of the cliff, and I grabbed at them with my hands as I went down. Several times I managed to catch hold of a branch, but it always broke off at once because I was so heavy and because I was falling so fast, and once I caught a thick branch with both hands and the tree leaned forward and I heard the snapping of the roots one by one until it came away from the cliff and I went on falling. Then it became darker because the sun and the day were in the fields far away at the top of the cliff, and as I fell I kept my eyes open and watched the darkness turn from gray-black to black, from black to jet black and from jet black to a pure liquid blackness which I could touch with my hands but which I could not see. But I went on falling, and it was so black that there was nothing anywhere and it was not any use doing anything or caring or thinking because of the blackness and because of the falling. It was not any use.

"You're better this morning. You're much better." It was the woman's voice again.

"Hallo."

"Hallo; we thought you were never going to get conscious."

Where am I?"

"In Alexandria; in hospital."

"How long have I been here?"

"Four days."

"What time is it?"

"Seven o'clock in the morning."

"Why can't I see?"

I heard her walking a little closer.

"Oh, we've just put a bandage around your eyes for a bit."

"How long for?"

"Just for a little while. Don't worry. You're fine. You were very lucky, you know."

I was feeling my face with my fingers but I couldn't feel it; I could only feel something else.

"What's wrong with my face?"

I heard her coming up to the side of my bed and I felt her hand touching my shoulder.

"You mustn't talk any more. You're not allowed to talk. It's bad for you. Just lie still and don't worry. You're fine."

I heard the sound of her footsteps as she walked across the floor and I heard her open the door and shut it again.

"Nurse," I said. "Nurse."

But she was gone.